Rachel's Promise

The Rachel Trilogy:
Book 1: *Rachel's Secret*
Book 2: *Rachel's Promise*
Book 3: *Rachel's Hope*

Rachel's Promise

SHELLY SANDERS

Second Story Press

Library and Archives Canada Cataloguing in Publication

Sanders, Shelly, 1964–, author
Rachel's promise / Shelly Sanders.

Issued in print and electronic formats.
ISBN 978-1-927583-14-2 (pbk.)
ISBN 978-1-927583-15-9 (epub)

I. Title.

PS8637.A5389R327 2013   jC813'.6   C2013-903867-1

C2013-903868-X

Editor: Sarah Swartz
Line Editor: Kathryn Cole
Design: Melissa Kaita
Map on page iv: Jenny Watson
Cover photos © iStockphoto

Printed and bound in Canada

*Second Story Press gratefully acknowledges the support of the Ontario Arts Council
and the Canada Council for the Arts for our publishing program. We acknowledge
the financial support of the Government of Canada through the Canada Book Fund.*

ONTARIO ARTS COUNCIL
CONSEIL DES ARTS DE L'ONTARIO
50 YEARS OF ONTARIO GOVERNMENT SUPPORT OF THE ARTS
50 ANS DE SOUTIEN DU GOUVERNEMENT DE L'ONTARIO AUX ARTS

Canada Council
for the Arts
Conseil des Arts
du Canada

MIX
Paper from
responsible sources
FSC® C004071
FSC
www.fsc.org

Published by
SECOND STORY PRESS
20 Maud Street, Suite 401
Toronto, ON M5V 2M5
www.secondstorypress.ca

In memory of my aunt, Anna (Nucia) Talan Rodkin, who shared with me precious memories and photos of her life in Russia and Shanghai. By remembering the history of our ancestors, we can ensure their stories never fade.

Rachel's Journey from Kishinev to Shanghai, 1903

PART ONE
Summer 1903

Become Christians and our brothers. If not, you have one year to go where you please. After that time there must not remain a single Jew in Russia...

—Bessarabetz [*daily Kishinev newspaper*],
June 18, 1903

I

Rachel and Nucia stood in the crowded aisle of the train headed to Vladivostok, pressed together like herrings stacked in tins at the fish market back home in their town of Kishinev. The air felt dry and hazy with tobacco fumes, and the steady beat of the train rolling along the tracks stuck in Rachel's head. Even when she fell asleep, Rachel could hear the train clanging.

"How much longer?" asked the little boy beside her.

Rachel felt a tap on her knee and turned to see Menahem, squeezed into a single seat beside her mother. He gazed at her with tired, red-rimmed eyes.

"Until the next stop or until we get to Vladivostok," she replied as she rubbed her churning stomach in circles.

"I want to get off now," Menahem complained.

She craned her neck to peer out through the smudged, dirty window at the trees passing by in a steady blur. The scenery hadn't changed in the two weeks since they'd begun their journey east across Russia. They were on their way to the port city of Vladivostok on the Sea of Japan, almost five thousand miles southeast of Kishinev. Kishinev had been the only home Rachel, Nucia, and Menahem had known. This town was located in a region called the Jewish Pale of Settlement. It was established by Tsar Catherine II in 1791 to rid the rest of Russia from Jewish competition and influence. And it was the only part of the Russian Empire where Jews were allowed to live.

Yet even within the Pale of Settlement, Jews experienced bloodshed from their Russian neighbors. Two months ago, Rachel's father had been killed during a brutal *pogrom*, a massacre against the Jews of the town that left Rachel's family and thousands of other people of their religion homeless. Now, they were fleeing Russia to get away from the unrelenting hostility towards Jews and the possibility of yet another massacre. From Vladivostok, the gateway to Asia and a prominent departure point for Russians, they would catch a steam ship to Shanghai, China, where they hoped to find work and save money for their final destination—America.

"We should be in Novonikolayevsk tonight," she said.

"Ohhhhhhh!" Menahem groaned and slouched down in his seat, jostling Rachel's mother, Ita.

The russet-brown wig Ita wore to cover her hair, the custom of every married observant Jewish woman, slid forward onto her brow. Ita didn't seem to notice but Nucia reached down and adjusted her mother's wig.

Rachel clenched her teeth and watched as Menahem, long faced, continued to squirm. Menahem was an orphan who was traveling with Rachel's family. "Sit still," she said tersely. She reached down, a difficult task in such a cramped space, and grasped his shoulder until he stopped fidgeting.

His dependence on her made Rachel uneasy, but she'd promised her friend Sergei to accompany seven-year-old Menahem from Russia to Shanghai or even to America. Yet she had no idea if their journey would be safe. Even when they arrived in Shanghai, they didn't know how Jews would be received, and they wouldn't be able to communicate with the Chinese. Fear squeezed her insides and made Rachel want to jump off the train and run back home to Sergei. She cared deeply for him though he was Russian, not Jewish, and a relationship between them was forbidden by both their religions.

Ita coughed, a sharp, mucus-filled sound that shook her entire body. She thrust both hands against her mouth, but the spasms were too violent to be silenced. Her face turned red and her eyes watered. She hunched her shoulders as if she wanted to disappear.

"Are you all right, Mother?" asked Nucia, Rachel's elder sister, removing her mushroom-colored shawl and wrapping it around her mother's neck. Nucia's long fingers deftly tucked the fabric until it stayed in place.

Ita nodded but continued to gag. Menahem put his small arm around her waist and rested his head against her side.

"I'll try to find the man on the train who sells tea," said Rachel. She peered up and down the aisle but saw only passengers.

"This is the worst Mother's been," said Nucia to Rachel. Nucia's face, which had always been thin, now looked angular, as if the skin had been snipped closely to her bones. She had just turned seventeen, while Rachel would be fifteen in November.

"I know." Rachel watched her mother, still hunched over in her seat. *I must be strong*, she vowed, recalling her father's face, and his lifeless body on the cold ground.

"This journey has been too hard on her," said Nucia.

"But we still have almost two weeks until we reach Vladivostok." Rachel looked up at her sister.

"What do you think we should do?" asked Nucia.

With a thoughtful expression, Rachel touched her amber pendant, which according to superstition had healing power, pulled the silver chain over her head and placed it around her mother's neck. She watched her mother for a moment and frowned. "What we really need to do is find some medicine."

"How?" asked Nucia.

"Ask other passengers if they have any medicine to spare."

"You mean ask complete strangers?" asked Nucia, shrinking back from Rachel.

"That's all we can do. There is no other way." Though she was the younger of the two, Rachel was often the one who had the practical solutions.

Nucia shook her head and turned away from her sister.

Rachel rolled her eyes and proceeded down the aisle, requesting cough medicine for her sick mother.

"No, I'm sorry," said a woman clutching a satchel to her chest.

"I'm afraid not," said a man, emptying out his pockets to check.

Halfway through the next compartment, when Rachel's throat had grown dry from asking, a middle-aged man said that he did have something. He unbuckled the satchel that hung over his shoulder and pulled out three brown lozenges, Hoffmann's Drops, a popular Russian medical panacea.

"Take them all," he said. "Sounds like your mother needs them more than I do."

"I can't tell you how much—"

"Say no more," said the man, settling back into his seat. "Just make sure you only give her one at a time. There's a fair bit of alcohol in them."

Rachel rushed back to her mother and slipped one into her mouth.

"Much…better," her mother said between coughs. After a few minutes of sucking on the drop, her cough began to subside and her eyelids drooped shut.

Rachel smiled with relief. She glanced at Nucia, but her red-faced sister hastily shifted her gaze from Rachel to the passing scenery.

上海

The train stopped abruptly in front of a small station. Rain drizzled down, darkening the wooden platform as it fell. A number of *Cossacks*, soldiers working for the Russian emperor, the Tsar, boarded the train as soon as it stopped. They were tough, bearded men with tall, dark fur hats, gray coats and trousers, and high black boots to their knees.

They were on the train to examine identity papers and exit visas. "Papers," they grunted, striding into each compartment.

"Where are your visas?" one Cossack asked a woman holding two small children. They sat two seats in front of Rachel.

"Everything in our house was destroyed," the woman said in a brittle voice. "My husband was killed. All our papers are gone."

"Off the train with you," ordered the Cossack. He seized the woman's shoulder and yanked her so hard she screamed.

Nucia grabbed Rachel's elbow and held on tight. Rachel wanted to look away but couldn't tear her gaze from the horrible scene unfolding.

"Please, let us stay. Let my children be safe." The woman fell to her knees and clasped her hands together. Her children clutched her shawl and cried.

Rachel covered her mouth and held her breath. The Cossack seized both children, one in each hand as if they were pails, and hauled them off the train. The mother, close behind him, sobbed and wailed for her children. Outside, on the dimly lit platform, the Cossack dropped the children and rubbed his hands together as if he'd just taken out the rubbish.

Menahem looked at Rachel with a fearful gaze that made her want to hold him tight. No wonder Sergei had become so attached to this sweet boy. Sergei had found him huddled amongst the remains of his shattered home during the Kishinev massacre. Menahem had watched his Jewish grandmother being beaten to death, leaving him orphaned. When threats of another riot arose, Sergei had taken Menahem from the orphanage to the train station, hoping that he could travel with Rachel to a safer place for Jews.

"Will they throw us off the train?" asked Menahem, watching the children on the platform, being comforted by their mother.

"No, we have our papers." Rachel handed the family's documents to the Cossack standing rigidly in the aisle beside her seat. Thank goodness the Kishinev orphanage had provided papers for Menahem. Nucia's hand still gripped her elbow.

The Cossack's muddy brown eyes studied each paper. He handed them back without a word and continued down the aisle.

"Where are we?" asked Menahem once the Cossacks had finished in their car, having thrown two other people off the train.

"We're in Omsk," she whispered.

Menahem stared at the wooden floor of the compartment.

Rachel looked at Menahem and thought to herself, *I don't know what to say to Menahem. I don't know how to reassure him that everything will be fine, when I don't know if this is true. How can I be responsible for a child when I can barely take care of myself?*

Rachel put her hand on Menahem's shoulder and watched the train crew jump to the ground with crude saws in their hands. They walked briskly to the forest behind the station. Rachel could see one man cutting down a tree for fuel. The other three were hidden behind the station. The sky grew dark and it started raining harder. All the Cossacks stepped off the train, gathered the people without identification papers, and roughly prodded them toward wagons attached to horses. The woman with two children turned her head to look back at the train. Her defeated eyes met Rachel's. Rachel clenched her jaw and tried to look in the opposite direction until she heard the horses cantering off. She could see the wagon pulling away, filled with unlucky people on their way to an unknown fate.

"Thirty-minute stop!" announced the *provodnitze*, the conductor, standing at the far end of the compartment. "Last stop before Novonikolayevsk."

Nucia finally let go of Rachel's elbow and knelt beside their mother.

A few vendors with pushcarts sold bread, milk, tea, and fish to passengers lining up on the platform. Rachel's mouth watered as she pictured a warm piece of bread slathered with fresh butter. But it had been her idea to wait until they reached Novonikolayevsk to eat in order to conserve their money. Now her stomach growled and she looked around to see if anyone had heard, but nobody paid any attention to her. Through the window, Rachel saw the train crew reappear, carting logs to feed the fire of the train.

"I have to go to the toilet," said Menahem.

Rachel grimaced. "Can't you wait until we get to Novonikolayevsk? The train is going to start soon."

"No...I really have to go badly."

"It's in the next compartment," said Nucia. She patted her mother's hair, stood, and dusted her wrinkled black skirt with the back of her hands.

Rachel grabbed Menahem's clammy hand and pulled him behind her. There was barely enough room to stand, let alone walk. As she passed men with broad girths, the rancid smells of perspiration and smoke assaulted her nose. She fanned the air in front of her with her hand but it didn't help at all.

"Just a few more minutes," she told Menahem when they joined the line to use the toilet.

He started to get fidgety, moving from one leg to the other. By the time his turn came, he almost collided with the girl who opened the door and walked out of the toilet, a narrow stall with a wooden bench that opened to a bucket below. Menahem rushed in and slammed the door.

"Wait here," Rachel told Menahem when he emerged. As soon as she entered the confining space, the stench hit her like a slap in the face. Rachel plugged her nose and imagined herself in a beautiful field of lilacs, a delicate fragrance filling the air. But no matter how hard she concentrated, she couldn't ignore the rank odor.

Rain came down hard as Rachel and Menahem made their way back to their compartment. It pummeled the roof of the train like stones flung against an empty pot. Rachel recalled that horrible April night when the riots against the Jews in Kishinev had begun. She, her mother, and Nucia had hid in the outhouse, where they heard heavy footsteps on the roof. She stopped suddenly, riveted by her own memories.

"Come on, Rachel."

Menahem's persistent voice jolted Rachel out of the past and back to the train. Shivers ran up and down her spine as she followed Menahem back to their compartment and squeezed in beside her sister.

The train lurched and then started to move again, gathering speed slowly. Rachel watched Menahem's eyelids drop, and then pop open as he tried to fight off his exhaustion. Within minutes, he fell asleep with his jaw slightly agape. Rachel saw how neatly Menahem fit against her mother. How natural they looked together. "Father always wanted a son," she said to Nucia, her voice breaking as she spoke.

上海

When they emerged from the train into the dim morning light, Rachel stopped and gazed at the green mountains rising high above the banks of Lake Baikal. The sapphire water turned into pounding white waves at the shore, the sound a welcome change from the monotonous clanging of the train.

She felt a tug at her sleeve and let Menahem pull her to the nearest vendor, a peasant dressed in a rumpled, stained shirt. As he handed her some figs, Rachel noticed that the underarm of his brown shirt had a dark circle from perspiration.

"Can we get some cheese?" asked Menahem.

Rachel's mouth watered when she eyed the small wheels of white and yellow cheese.

"Only seven *kopecks*," said the peasant.

Rachel looked at the money in her hand and shook her head. "We cannot afford such a luxury as cheese. Just the figs and some bread."

Menahem nodded and looked away.

The peasant shrugged and filled Rachel's basket with bread.

Rachel counted her money carefully and handed it to the peasant. Just then the bell announced the train's departure from Irkutsk. She squeezed Menahem's hand as they scurried back to their compartment.

As soon as Menahem devoured his food, he fell asleep. His head rested against the dirt-streaked window.

"He's too thin," said Ita, now sitting across from him. She sounded weak and raspy. "Too small for a boy of seven."

"He wants cheese but it's too expensive." Rachel took a small bite of her bread to make it last.

"We will get him some cheese in Vladivostok." Ita thrust her chin forward, looking more determined than Rachel had seen in months.

"But we need to ration our money," said Nucia.

"He's a growing boy and I haven't been very hungry since our journey began." She coughed suddenly and covered her mouth with her hand.

"How are you feeling today?" asked Rachel.

"Don't worry about me." Her mother smiled thinly. "I'll be fine."

Rachel nodded and, from her aisle seat, surveyed the compartment of Jewish refugees. A young family with six children had squeezed into the seats in front of them, and five men stood in the aisle. Directly across from her, four men slumped in their seats, asleep and snoring noisily. All of them wore skullcaps and had long side locks.

"Too much vodka," said a girl sitting diagonally across from Rachel. She had impossibly long eyelashes and bronze-colored skin.

"Is that why they're snoring so loudly?" asked Rachel.

"I think they'd snore whether they had vodka or not."

"Oh, dear," sighed Rachel. She pulled the wooden fragment of her father's violin, all that had remained of his prized instrument, from the cloth pouch that hung over her shoulder. She rubbed the darker polished side with her finger.

"Where are you from?" asked the girl in Yiddish, leaning over the side of her seat.

"Kishinev. And you?"

"Novonikolayevsk. My husband and I are on our way to Shanghai."

"Are you married?" Rachel couldn't hide her surprise—this girl couldn't be more than fifteen.

She blushed. "My husband and I have known each other all of our lives."

Rachel's mother coughed again, more violently, for several seconds. Rachel gave her another drop and watched until the coughing eased.

"How long have you been married?" asked Rachel.

The girl giggled and brought her hand to her mouth.

Sadness yanked at Rachel's heart. This girl reminded her of Chaia, her best friend, still at the Kishinev hospital, in a coma since the pogrom.

"Three months." Her gaze fell on a tall, skinny boy walking down the aisle. His trousers hung loose around his waist and the bottom three buttons of his shirt were undone. "Here's Isaac now. He gets so restless sitting."

Isaac inserted himself into the seat beside the girl, his bony knees sticking up awkwardly.

"This is—" she turned her head toward Rachel and brought her hand to her mouth again. "I'm sorry, I don't know your name."

"Rachel."

She placed her hand against her chest. "I'm Shprintze and this is Isaac."

He nodded affably at Rachel.

"Where are you going?" he asked her, his tone warm but formal.

Rachel glanced over her shoulder at her mother and Menahem, sleeping fitfully. "We have tickets to Vladivostok. We want to purchase steerage tickets on a ship to Shanghai."

Isaac and Shprintze exchanged smiles.

"That's our plan as well," said Isaac, looking again at Rachel. "To get out of Russia."

"Isaac decided we should leave and bought our train tickets the next day," added Shprintze.

"There's nothing for us Jews here in Russia," said Isaac.

"But our families have stayed in Russia," added Shprintze. "My mother refuses to leave, even after…" She lowered her head and sniffed back tears.

Rachel turned away. A couple of minutes later, when Rachel glanced back at Shprintze, she saw that Isaac had his arm draped around his young wife. Rachel's insides fluttered with envy, seeing how he showed his support and love for her in public, something she and Sergei were never able to do.

"We hope her parents will come when we're settled," explained Isaac.

Shprintze lifted her head and nodded. "I'm terrified about being a refugee and living in a different country," she said to Rachel. "Aren't you?"

"I try not to think about it too much."

Shprintze smiled wanly at Rachel, settled into the crook of Isaac's arm, and closed her eyes. Isaac sat perfectly still and erect, as if afraid to disturb his wife.

Rachel sat back and touched the fragment of her father's violin again. She pictured him playing it in their small home in Kishinev, his attention focused on his rapidly moving bow. Rachel strained to recall the sound of the strings.

2

Sergei knelt down and embraced his eight-year-old sister, Natalya. Her little body shook in his arms. His mother hovered over him, dabbing her eyes with a muslin square.

In the vestibule of their home, on the second floor of a four-storey building in Kishinev, stale cigarette smoke tinged the air. All the shutters were closed, leaving the flat dark and dreary, though it was a sunny June afternoon.

"I wish you didn't have to go," said Natalya. She burrowed her face into his shoulder. When she lifted her head, she accidentally bumped against Sergei's jaw, still tender from his father's fist.

Sergei jerked his head back and winced.

"It still hurts?" said Natalya.

"Just a little."

"Your eye isn't healed yet, either," said his mother. She squinted at his swollen, yellowish-gray left eye.

16

"I'll be fine," said Sergei.

"Come, Natalya," said their mother, gently pulling the girl away from her brother. "Sergei has to get to the train station."

Sergei slowly got to his feet. "Are you sure—"

His mother nodded and crossed her hands over her heart. "You'll let me know where you are?"

"Of course," he answered.

His mother stepped back, her arm around Natalya, weeping softly into the sleeve of her navy dress.

The sound of heavy footsteps marching up the front steps made Sergei's stomach lurch. The door burst open and his father appeared, his bloodshot eyes seething at Sergei.

"You're nothing but a coward!" yelled his father in a slurred voice. His long, dark whiskers were tangled, his hair matted and his clothing stunk of smoke and brandy. Since losing his position as Chief of Police after the pogrom, he'd taken to filling his days with alcohol at local taverns.

Sergei clenched his teeth and tried to squeeze past him into the corridor, but his father grabbed his ear and yanked him back.

"Let me go!" said Sergei.

"Take your hands off him, Aleksandr," cried Sergei's mother.

Natalya whimpered and tugged at her father's sleeve. Her mother pulled her away.

"If you leave, you are weak like a worm. If you stay, you will be strong like a bear," said Sergei's father. He released Sergei's ear and staggered backwards, falling against the corridor wall.

"I'd rather be a humble worm than a clumsy bear." Sergei squared his broad shoulders with his father's and glared down at him with dark, scalding eyes.

A confused expression crept across his father's ruddy face. Sergei smelled his father's fetid breath and scowled.

"Go, Sergei," said his mother. "Make haste, just go."

Sergei swallowed and watched his father sway back and forth from the alcohol he'd been drinking all day. Sergei picked up his satchel, which contained a clean shirt and trousers, soap, and his sketchpad and pencils, gave his mother one final embrace and scurried down the corridor.

"Coward!" his father called out when Sergei reached the stairs.

Outside on the streets of Kishinev, anger spread through Sergei, as he passed abandoned and demolished shops from the Easter pogrom. A Jewish bookstore, where the glass had been shattered, had been boarded up. A candle shop that had been set on fire remained a charred ruin. And the sidewalks, once lively and full of people, were practically empty except for a few men standing outside a tavern and a newspaper vendor selling his wares.

Walking by the newsstand, Sergei could read the headlines of the popular anti-Jewish Kishinev newspaper, *Bessarabetz*. It was filled with hate propaganda, such as falsely blaming the Jews for the death of Christians. The lies in these "news" stories had incited the Kishinev pogrom, a massacre of its Jewish population and the destruction of their property.

The riots had continued for over three days because the police had not intervened. Viacheslav von Plehve, the Interior Minister in charge of police in all of Russia, had instructed the local police not to stop the rioting Russian civilians. In effect, he had allowed the pogrom in Kishinev that had injured and killed many Jews and destroyed their homes and stores. Numerous survivors had now fled from Kishinev. If it hadn't been for Plehve, fumed Sergei, Kishinev might still be the same today. Menahem would have his grandmother and Rachel wouldn't have been forced to leave. It was obvious to Sergei that Plehve was very powerful and that he hated the Jews. *I will not rest until von Plehve and his cloak of hatred are gone forever,* he promised himself.

At Aleksandrov Street, Sergei stopped and stared across the road at the Jewish part of town where the pogrom had begun on Easter Sunday. In his mind he could still see images of people, beaten until their bodies were mangled lumps of bloody flesh. His ears were still filled with the sounds of grown men pleading for their lives, women and babies screaming, their voices fading into the air. Though he himself was a Christian, he had been filled with revulsion.

Sergei remembered hearing a small boy's cry. He had found Menahem. After witnessing his grandmother being bludgeoned to death, he had been hiding amongst the rubble of his home. Sergei thought about the Jewish boy in whom he had taken an interest and who had become like a younger brother to him. He clenched his fists as he remembered how he had taken Menahem to the Kishinev orphanage and how hard it had been to leave him there, even though he had often gone to visit him.

As Sergei turned from Aleksandrov Street, the memories and noises thrashed inside his head. When he reached the train station, Sergei recalled the chaotic scene—two weeks earlier—when many Jews had flooded the tracks, fleeing the threat of yet another pogrom. He'd taken Menahem from the orphanage, so that he would not have to witness more violence, and brought him to the train station where Rachel and her family were leaving for Shanghai. He begged Rachel to take Menahem with them. Sergei remembered the sadness in Menahem's face and the fear in Rachel's voice as they said goodbye to him, not knowing if they would ever see each another again.

Sergei winced and tried again to thrust these recollections from his mind. He could not. They were as entrenched in his brain as deeply as his feelings for his sister and mother—and his memory of Mikhail. Mikhail had been his closest friend. When he was found dead in February, it was the Jews who had been blamed, even though there'd been no evidence. In the end, Mikhail's uncle and cousin were found guilty of the crime. But that didn't stop the pogrom against the Jews.

Now he bought a one-way ticket to Saint Petersburg, in the heart of Russia, nine hundred miles north on the Gulf of Finland, and found a window seat near the back of the train just five minutes before the departure time. A group of university students, distinctive in their blue embroidered collars, three-cornered hats, and gild swords hanging at their sides, dashed into his car just as the train rumbled to a start. Sergei noticed they weren't much older than him. He focused on the scenery rolling past: silvery birch trees in full bloom; dark green spruce and fir trees. In the distance, blurred hills rose to meet the hazy sky. And somewhere beyond these hills, far away, Rachel and Menahem were on their way to Shanghai, unrelated by blood yet bound together by their Jewish heritage.

Sergei smiled faintly as he thought about Rachel. He imagined her infectious laugh and saw her auburn air falling past her shoulders when she undid her braid and combed her locks with her hand.

"Stupid Jew!" Sergei shuddered as he remembered the

Russian girls shouting these words at Rachel as they hit and kicked her. When he saw this scene, he had intervened, chasing the girls away from Rachel. He caught Rachel before she collapsed to the ground. A lump rose from her pale forehead and blood stained her face. But when he looked into her soulful green eyes, he fell for her.

"We can't be seen together," Rachel had protested when he tried to kiss her some time later. They'd gone for a walk in the spring. The ground had been wet and covered with mushrooms but they'd found a dry spot at the edge of the river. "If anyone saw you with me, they'd kill me and maybe even you."

Rachel had good reason to be afraid. Sergei's father was the chief of police and not only did he dislike Jews, he had encouraged the riots and made no attempt to stop them—just like von Plehve. Still, Sergei persisted with Rachel, kissing her again. His heart sped up as he remembered how she'd finally returned his affection, kissing him back.

"We will see each other again, I promise," Sergei had told her the last day, when he brought Menahem to the train station to join her family.

"We'll see you in Shanghai or in America," she'd replied with certainty. "Things will be different, better. Meanwhile I promise to take care of Menahem."

Sergei had held onto Rachel's reassuring words. They'd kept him going over the last couple of weeks, giving him hope when nothing good seemed possible.

Students' laughter jolted Sergei from his memories of Rachel. He watched them with a twinge of envy, then forced himself to listen to the rhythmic sound of the train rolling along the tracks, until it filled his head and blocked out the boisterous noise of the students. But as he watched Kishinev disappear through the window, his father's words echoed in his head— *coward, coward, coward…*

上海

Sergei strode onto the platform at the Vitebsky station in Petersburg. After four long days and nights on the train, he was grateful to feel solid ground beneath his feet. He threw his satchel over his shoulder and followed the crowd down the track toward a wide opening that led into the mammoth station. A single ticket booth opened and a few people sat on benches waiting for trains to arrive. The sound of shoes echoed sharply in the vast terminal.

Though it was almost midnight, he could see yellowish light through the semi-circular windows at the top of the building. Sergei rushed to the door at the front of the station and made his way to the street, which seemed eerily bright, as if it were late afternoon—the white nights of Saint Petersburg. Sergei had read about Petersburg in June and July, when night became indistinguishable from day in this northern-most city. The buttery sky set off the area like a brilliant canvas, with buildings and streets illuminated under the soft light. Fluffy clouds hung overhead, adorning the sky with their purplish-blue haze.

Standing in front of the train station at the corner of Zagorodny Avenue and the Vvedensky Canal, Sergei pivoted on one foot, trying to decide which way to go. It occurred to him that, for the first time in his life, he was completely alone. Nobody expected him and he had nowhere to be. A strange mixture of anticipation, fear, and relief flooded him as he began

Nevsky Prospekt. Divided in the center by trolley tracks, the Nevsky Prospekt appeared to be three times broader than the widest street in Kishinev. An arcade filled the lower level of the market, which supported an open gallery on the upper level. An icon depicting Saint Nicholas had been painted on the arcade's vaulted ceiling.

The peasants vanished into the crowd of vendors getting ready for the day, setting up displays of a vast array of items—bread, *pirozhki,* incense, dried fruit, long strings of dried mushrooms, figs, and *kvass,* Sergei's favorite drink, made from bread. Reaching into his leather pouch, Sergei pulled out a few kopecks and bought some pirozhki, which he devoured in seconds. He counted out three more kopecks.

"One glass," he told the kvass vendor, a short man with wide shoulders and a narrow waist. The man grunted, took Sergei's kopecks, and poured a tall glass of the drink.

Sergei tipped his head back and sent the liquid down his throat. Then he set the glass down on the man's wooden cart and continued through the market, passing a Cossack. In a corner, a policeman stood with a grim expression, watching out for trouble. Sergei thought about his father and the other policemen in Kishinev, who'd done nothing to stop the deadly riots, and his stomach hardened.

Sergei strolled in the direction of a fish stall, where the fish were piled like cordwood. Fishermen, dressed in animal skins, with weather-beaten faces, stood over their merchandise, examining the shoppers with shrewd expressions.

Farther on, he came upon vendors with mounds of the biggest fruits and vegetables he'd ever seen—potatoes that wouldn't even fit in his hand, perfectly round scarlet cherries, melons as big as his head, and so many oranges, they seemed as common as sacks of hay.

"Read today's *Novoe Vremia*," a young boy on the corner cried out, waving the newspaper in the air. "Only three kopecks."

Seeing the bold headlines reminded Sergei of the false news in the Kishinev newspaper that had ignited the riots, blaming the Jews for the murder of his friend. He thought about Rachel and her steadfast determination to become a journalist and to write the truth. He remembered how strong she'd been after her father had been killed and her home destroyed. He admired her courage after the riots were over.

Colorful shawls, intricate lace, and pewter-cross icons lay neatly displayed in booths along the way. Sergei fingered the cross that had hung from his neck all of his life, honoring his faith. He kept walking until he reached another canal. He stared at the marshy water for a moment, and then pulled the chain over his head. In one swift motion, he threw it into the canal and walked away without looking back.

上海

The road widened, impressive buildings with columns and arches stood on both sides of the street, painted in colors that seemed to have been inspired by foods—gingerbread brown, lemon yellow, cherry red, blueberry, raspberry, and lime green. Horse-drawn carriages hurried by in both directions, making familiar clip-clop sounds as they moved past Sergei. At one corner, he came upon the Hotel Europe, a four-storey stone building that looked fit for the Tsar. Two men in waistcoats stood in front of the hotel.

Sergei continued across the street, his head turning from side to side absorbing every sight and sound. So many people spoke in languages he'd never heard before. He couldn't help but gape at a couple with white-blond hair, a petite Chinese woman in a shiny silk robe, and a group of men with tea-colored skin and straight black hair.

Sergei's feet were tired and swollen from walking, and his head throbbed with exhaustion. When he came to a long, low apartment building, he shuffled through the narrow ground-floor corridor and found the landlord's door. Taking a deep breath, he knocked.

A sturdy woman with heavily lidded eyes opened the door.

"I'm looking for a room to rent," said Sergei, in the deepest tone he could muster.

Her gaze roamed from his feet to his head. "You have a job?" she asked.

"Not yet, I just moved here."

She shook her head. "Can't take anyone without employment."

"Please—"

The door slammed shut and Sergei felt as if she'd punched him in the stomach. He stood in front of the closed door for a moment, temporarily paralyzed. A few seconds later, he recovered his nerve and continued his hunt.

"I only rent to families," said a gruff man at the next apartment building, giving Sergei a skeptical look.

"But I'm quiet and neat," pleaded Sergei.

"To me it looks like you know where to find trouble." The man stared at Sergei's black eye.

"It's not what—"

The man smirked and shut the door in Sergei's face.

Sergei trudged to the next apartment building and knocked on the landlord's door.

"We're full," said the little man who answered.

"Wait!" he cried.

The door shut before the word jumped out of his mouth.

Sergei continued down the street and turning the corner, arrived on a side street that came off the Nevsky Prospekt. He discovered a tall, narrow wooden hostel that looked as rickety as some of the houses in Kishinev's Jewish ghetto, where Rachel had lived. The disparity between this building and the colorful ones he'd seen only blocks from here, startled Sergei.

Sergei walked into the decrepit hostel and noticed the smell of dirty feet. He glanced down at the wooden plank floor, expecting to see boots strewn all around, but there were none. A stooped man with thinning gray hair stood behind a wood counter in the cramped entry hall.

To the right, a young woman descended the staircase, straightening her long gray skirt as she promenaded past Sergei and out the door.

"Thirty kopecks a night," the man growled. "Steam bath and outhouse are in the courtyard."

"I'll give you fifty kopecks for two nights."

The man folded his burly arms across his chest and shook his head.

Sergei's heart thumped, but he steadied his gaze on the man, shrugged, and turned to leave.

"Fifty-five for two nights," said the man when Sergei's hand touched the door.

Sergei reached into his pouch and carefully took out the money.

A musty odor accompanied Sergei as he headed up to his room on the fourth floor. Through the paper-thin doors along the corridor, he heard a child crying, a woman yelling, and a heated conversation between two men.

His narrow room contained a cot and an oil lamp perched on a small, round table. When he sat down on the bed, a rat scurried across the floor and disappeared underneath the door. Sergei grimaced and looked up at the narrow window above the bed, where the white night streamed in. As he collapsed onto the lumpy bed, he wondered whether his mother and sister would be all right without him. He also wondered if Menahem would ever forgive him for sending him away, if he'd ever see him and Rachel again. Then he drifted into a restless sleep.

3

Mounted Cossacks lined both sides of the tracks when the train pulled into Khabarovsk—the last stop before Vladivostok—igniting a nervous murmur throughout the compartment. Rachel craned her neck to look out the window. The sleek horses stood motionless, like the uniformed men sitting tall and rigidly astride them.

The door at the far end of the train compartment opened suddenly, letting in a gust of hot air. A formidable looking Cossack, in a long, green-belted coat appeared.

"Exit visas!" he barked.

Rachel's fingers fumbled as she opened the pouch that hung from her mother's waist.

"What's wrong?" her mother asked feebly.

"Don't worry, we just have to show our papers proving we're allowed to leave Russia," answered Rachel. She took the neatly folded documents, issued at the Kishinev train station, from the pouch and clutched them in her hand.

The Cossack moved through the compartment, checking papers methodically, grunting occasionally.

"Where are your travel papers?" said the Cossack to a young man sitting in front of Rachel.

"I don't have them," answered the man, who had long, curly hair.

"Why not?" demanded the Cossack.

"Because I was conscripted into the army," said the man, referring to the common practice of the government forcing young men to join the military. "I was supposed to report to the army next week."

"But Solomon, you told me you talked to someone in the army," cried the red-haired woman beside the man. "You said you didn't have to join, that we could leave Russia."

"I'm sorry," he said quietly, "I don't have permission to leave Russia."

"Come with me," ordered the Cossack. He grabbed the young man's collar and dragged him from the train.

"You can't take him. I have nobody else!" cried the woman. She stood in the train's aisle, her shoulders limp. "How will I find you, Solomon?"

"Send your letters to the Russian army in Vladivostok," answered the Cossack brusquely.

"No, Solomon, no…there must be something we can do!" screamed the woman. She lunged forward.

Isaac rushed to the woman and held her back. "You must stay on the train," he told her. "That's what Solomon wants for you."

The woman struggled to escape Isaac's grasp, but he tightened his hold on her.

"What's wrong, Rachel?" asked Menahem. He climbed onto her lap.

"Just stay quiet," said Rachel.

Outside, Solomon, along with a few other men removed from the train, was shackled to the Cossacks' horses. "Solomon doesn't belong in the army," sobbed the woman. "He'd never hurt anyone."

"He might not have to fight," said Isaac, letting go of her. "We're not at war right now."

"But I don't know what to do, where to go…"

"I'm sure he'll find you as quickly as he can," said Shprintze.

"You really think so?" The woman looked at Shprintze with swollen, red eyes. Her cheeks and sharp, beak-like nose were covered in pockmarks.

"I do."

Holding on to Menahem, Rachel bit her lip and stared out the window at the departing Cossacks and their newly acquired soldiers.

上海

After more than three weeks and three thousand miles on the train from Kishinev, Rachel and her family arrived in Vladivostok, the principal seaport city in southeast Russia. Rachel rested her hand on her queasy stomach, turned from the window, and gazed around the train compartment. It seemed quieter than it had been during the whole journey. Men who had talked loudly with bold hand gestures stood silently now. Children slouched in their seats, worn out from the long ride.

Exhausted women had fixed dirty babushkas on their heads and wore disheveled, unwashed clothing.

The woman whose husband had been taken away sat hunched over, like a wilted tulip.

"I feel terrible for her," whispered Rachel to Nucia. "She's all alone."

"There's nothing we can do," said Nucia, braiding their mother's hair. "We can hardly afford to take care of Menahem."

"I know." Rachel took a deep breath and looked away from the woman. *Father would not want us turning our backs on anyone, but Nucia is right. If we want to survive, we must put ourselves first.*

Isaac took Shprintze's hand, pulled her to her feet, and they joined the swarm of people gathering in the aisle to get off the train.

Rachel, catching the loving gaze between Isaac and Shprintze, smiled and felt her heart swell with hope. She fingered the violin fragment in her pouch. This was the one remnant of her former life. Then she wrapped her hand around the journal Sergei had given to her and, clutching Menahem's hand, stepped with renewed confidence into the growing throng of people shuffling toward the door.

When she finally walked onto the concrete platform, Rachel flinched when she heard all the noises around her: people shouting, whistles blowing sharply, and the clang of another train's arrival. Voices ricocheted in the vast building, which had a higher roof than anything Rachel had ever seen. Soot and cigarette smoke filled the air.

Ita coughed fitfully, her whole body wracked in spasms. Nucia put her arm around their mother, who seemed to have shrunk during their journey. Rachel focused on her mother. The blood vessels in her face had burst, leaving red, squiggly lines that crisscrossed her skin like embroidered thread. Rachel took a deep breath and trailed behind Isaac and Shprintze as they moved toward a doorway at the far end of the station. Rachel's family and Isaac and Shprintze had bonded on the train. Now they promised to stay together for the next leg of their trip to Shanghai.

"Can we get something to drink, Rachel?" asked Menahem. "I'm thirsty."

"We'll stop for a drink before going to the steerage office," she said, moving toward the door that led to the street.

The warm air outside hit Rachel like a blanket. Beads of perspiration ran down her face and neck. She twisted her head around when a ship's horn blew and saw the Golden Horn Bay, named for its horn shape, which opened to the Sea of Japan. Vladivostok lay on the hills at the head of the bay. Rachel stared out at the steamships gliding across the water. She wondered where they were going and what kind of stories their passengers had to tell.

"I'm thirsty and tired," Menahem repeated, his small face dripping with sweat.

"Stop complaining," said Rachel.

"Let me help," said Isaac, giving Rachel a sympathetic smile. Though he and Shprintze had only known Rachel's family a short time, they were united by the same goals—getting far away from Russia and its dangerous pogroms, and seeking refuge in Shanghai. As Jews, they had all suffered persecution in Russia and were united by their experiences. He released Shprintze's hand, crouched down and beckoned for Menahem to climb on his shoulders.

Menahem scrambled onto Isaac's back. Isaac stood and Menahem, his arms wrapped around Isaac's neck, grinned.

"Now, let's find some food," Rachel said, in a strong tone that belied her own uncertainty. "We'll feel better once we've filled our stomachs." She looked right, then left, and led the way across the street where people strode purposefully along the wooden-planked sidewalk.

Kerosene street lamps and tall scrawny trees lined the dirt road, and horse-drawn carriages, carrying well-dressed people, sped past. Walking along a street that ran parallel to the bay, they came to a bright yellow five-storey building adorned with a large sign: The Grand Hotel. Seeing a woman in a blue silk dress with a wide-brimmed hat emerge from the hotel's entrance made Rachel feel even more dirty and tired.

They continued on, turning left at Svetlanskaya Street, which appeared to be a main street, sure to have restaurants. Shprintze caught up to Rachel and the two of them walked ahead of everyone else. Rachel's legs, weak from almost a month of train travel, burned with fatigue as they climbed the street that rose above them. She paused, rested her hands on her thighs, and continued. At the top of the hill, they came to a public garden where vendors were selling *blini*, oranges, dried fruit, fish, cheese, bread, and tea. Menahem and Isaac rushed to a vendor selling black bread, with Rachel and Shprintze close behind them. Rachel bought four thick slices of bread, slathered with butter, two pieces of white cheese, bigger than Menahem's hands, four perfectly round oranges, and four glasses of cold tea. They all sat under a tall linden tree in the garden, their legs spread out on the lush, cool grass. A slight breeze cleansed their faces with salty sea air.

"I think food tastes better outside, like this," said Nucia, after she had eaten her bread.

"Me too," said Menahem.

Ita nibbled at her bread but did not eat much more than a corner. Rachel anxiously watched her mother. She noticed how her breathing seemed labored and feared that the journey to Shanghai would leave her even weaker.

"I'm so hungry, I'd eat anything," said Nucia, before putting a piece of cheese in her mouth.

"Would you eat dirt?" asked Menahem, with a mouth full of bread.

"Maybe not dirt."

He looked around the garden. "How about leaves from a tree?"

Nucia made a face and shook her head.

"What about grass?" Menahem pulled a clump of grass from the ground and held it out to her.

"No."

"But you said you would eat anything."

"He's right," said Isaac laughing. "That's what you said."

"It's just an expression," said Nucia to Menahem. "I didn't actually mean *anything*."

Shprintze chuckled softly and Isaac smiled. Ita's cheeks flushed unnaturally bright with color. She coughed, a wet, throaty sound that brought an abrupt end to their laughter.

Rachel rubbed her temple and sighed. She peeled the mottled skin of the orange with her fingers. As she listened to her mother cough, again and again, her heart sank.

上海

Rachel opened her eyes slowly and rubbed her head. A dull aching stiffness had settled in her body from being outside all night. She shivered and gazed at the people waiting outside the Vladivostok steerage office, located in the basement of a large brick building near the dock. There were hundreds gathered, mostly Jews fleeing Russian pogroms, in their traditional dark clothing—women with scarves covering their hair and bearded men with tall hats and long coats—clutching their few possessions in bags and baskets.

Overhead, wispy white clouds met in the center of the sky where a pink ribbon of light emerged. The gray water looked darker as it neared the misty horizon. Close to the wooden dock, white edges broke through the murky surface. Rachel shaded her eyes with her hand; Shanghai lay somewhere out there, past the horizon, sixteen hundred miles away. They'd come so far, yet they were still in Russia. And they still had a long way to go.

Menahem sprawled out behind Rachel, his head resting against her back. She ran her fingers through his hair, which had grown long, almost to his collar, and had become damp with the humid morning air. Her mother and Nucia gazed at the crowd impassively, and Shprintze, her body curled into a ball, lay like a child with her head in Isaac's lap.

"It smells like dead fish here," said Menahem, yawning as he spoke. "Will the ship smell this bad?"

Rachel wrinkled her nose to avoid the awful stench rising from the inky-blue water that thrashed against the dock. "It will be fine, the smell won't come through the ship," she said, attempting to sound positive. She stood and stared at the black steamship, *Simbirsk*, named for a city in western Russia, looming like a dark cave. Her stomach muscles clenched tightly as she examined the windowless underside of the vessel.

The agent walked past the people in line and unlocked the door to the steerage office.

"Wake up." Isaac ruffled Shprintze's hair.

Shprintze sat up and stretched her arms over her head.

"You wouldn't waken if a rook cawed right beside us," said Isaac.

"That's not true. I barely slept last night with all the noise around here."

Isaac chortled.

Menahem scrambled to his feet. His hair stuck up oddly at the side of his head, which he tilted back to look at the ship. "That yellow and black pipe sticking out of the boat looks like a lit cigarette."

"That's where the steam comes out," Rachel explained.

A shadow crossed Menahem's face.

"This is going to be exciting," said Rachel quickly. "Like an adventure in a book! Only we get to have the adventure. A new country! New people!"

"I don't feel good," said Menahem.

"Nobody here feels good," snapped Rachel, regretting her words as soon as they flew out of her mouth.

"Take my hand," offered Shprintze. Menahem slipped his hand into hers.

Seeing how easily Menahem accepted Shprintze's hand, made Rachel feel ashamed. She felt as if she were letting Sergei down by not being more patient with Menahem.

Rachel pressed her lips together and began moving forward with the crowd, toward the steerage office. With every step she took, Rachel's stomach tightened.

"How many passengers?" asked the agent when Rachel and Nucia stood in the dimly lit steerage office, in front of his desk.

"Four." Nucia glanced at Rachel as she spoke, as if she were seeking approval for her response.

"One child and three adults," added Rachel.

Menahem let go of Shprintze and stood beside Rachel.

The agent squinted and examined their faces, stopping when he looked at Rachel's mother. "You don't look well enough to travel," he said to her.

"I feel fine," said Ita in a hoarse voice.

He shook his head. "They won't let you stay in Shanghai if you're ill."

"She's just tired," said Rachel.

"Looks sick to me," said the agent. "Next." He gestured for Rachel to step out of the way.

"But you can't do this," said Rachel. She moved in closer to the agent until her face was just inches from his. "We've come so far. There's nothing for us in Russia."

"All passengers must be healthy," he replied impatiently. "Now move away so I can take the next passengers."

Rachel took Menahem's hand and stepped to the side. She watched as Isaac paid for the tickets for himself and Shprintze.

"What are we going to do?" said Nucia, her eyes darting from her mother to Rachel.

"I'm sorry," said Ita, like a helpless child who'd been reprimanded.

"It's not your fault," said Rachel. "But we have to think of a way to get on this ship."

"Why won't they let us go?" asked Menahem.

"Quiet," said Rachel. "I need to think."

Menahem moved from Rachel to Nucia. Rachel watched as people continued moving forward, either paying for their passage, or being rejected. One family was turned away because the child had a patch over his eye, another because the father limped.

"What are you going to do, Rachel?" asked Shprintze.

"I don't see any way around this, unless your mother stays in Russia," said Isaac.

"No. Our family has already been broken," said Rachel. "We are going to stay together and we're all getting on that ship."

"How?" asked Isaac.

Rachel ignored his question and marched toward a young man standing alone in the line. He had long side locks. "Are you traveling alone?" she asked him.

He nodded.

"If I give you the money, will you buy an extra adult ticket for me?"

He lowered his chin. "Why?"

"Because the ticket agent has mistaken my mother's exhaustion for sickness and won't sell her a ticket."

"What if he asks to see the person I'm buying the ticket for?"

"Then we won't get the ticket, but please try, please."

"I can pretend to be with you," said Shprintze, coming toward Rachel.

"But he'll recognize you," said Rachel.

"Maybe not." Shprintze removed the shawl from her head, which identified her as a married woman, and rummaged through her sack, pulling out a pair of spectacles. "These were my mother's," she said, placing them on her face. "Now we are brother and sister," she said to the young man.

"I can't believe you're the same person!" said Rachel.

"How can I say no to you?" said the young man with a hint of a smile. He opened his palms to the sky.

"Thank you, thank you," said Rachel. She handed the young man enough *rubles* for an adult fare and stepped back.

Rachel re-joined her family and Isaac, and watched from the corner of her eye as Shprintze and the man approached the ticket agent. The agent crumpled his brow for a second, asked a couple of questions, took the man's money, and handed him two tickets. Rachel grabbed Nucia's hand and squeezed it so tight that Nucia cried out. Shprintze strode past Rachel and slipped the ticket into her hand.

Now Rachel led her mother off to the side of the line, out of sight of the ticket agent. "Mother you wait here while we get in line to buy our tickets," said Rachel.

Shprintze wrapped her arm around Rachel's mother and nodded for Rachel, Menahem, and Nucia to go. The line seemed to move more slowly than before. Rachel worried that there would be no space left by the time they reached the ticket agent.

When they finally stood before the agent, Rachel felt sure he could hear her heart pounding. "Two adults and one child," she said.

The agent scrutinized her, Nucia, and Menahem. "What about your sick mother?" he asked.

"She's staying in Russia," said Rachel.

The agent grunted and asked for their names and places of birth, which he recorded in a large book. He scooped up her money and handed her three tickets. The agent told Rachel and

Nucia they were in Group A of steerage and that they should proceed to the landing stage at the dock.

"We're going to Shanghai!" Rachel said in an incredulous tone when they returned to their mother and Shprintze.

Ita looked numb with disbelief. Shprintze threw her arms around Rachel and Menahem. They held each other close, as if they'd known one another forever.

I hope we are never separated, that we never have to say goodbye. I don't think I can bear losing another friend, thought Rachel to herself.

At the dock, hundreds of other steerage passengers stood rigidly with distant expressions on their faces, waiting to board the ship. The humidity rose faster than water coming to a boil in a samovar. Rachel's clothing stuck to her back and shoulders as beads of perspiration dripped from her forehead. She felt tired and thirsty. And nervous.

She had never set foot on a ship before, a ship that would take them far away from land, from Russia, from her father whom they had buried in Kishinev. Rachel began to worry about the ship sinking, taking all the passengers to the bottom of the sea. She remembered swimming with Nucia in the River Byk when they were little, how she'd held her breath until her head grew dizzy and her cheeks seemed as if they would burst.

Rachel peered at the ship that would soon hold their lives within its hull. She squeezed Menahem's hand and glanced back at the port of Vladivostok, rising above them in the hills, marking the end of Russia for them.

4

Sergei woke up scratching. His back, his head, his neck—every part of his skin itched. He bolted upright and scraped at his neck until it bled, trying to get rid of the prickly feeling, as if something were crawling all over him—yet he saw nothing.

As he dropped his feet onto the dirty wood floor, he noticed rat droppings scattered across the ground. Sergei jumped up, yanked the door open, and ran down the stairs.

The courtyard stank of beer and filth. He breathed through his mouth and entered the steam bath behind the adjacent hotel, scratching his right side vigorously. A man with a large nose etched with broken blood vessels sat on the only bench getting undressed. Sergei removed his shirt and sat down, still scratching.

"Bed bugs," said the man. He fumbled with the buttons on his shirt.

"What?"

"You had company in your bed last night. That's why you're scratching."

Sergei puckered his brow.

"Hostel's full of them, they're so small you can't see them, but they're there." He stood up and strolled to the door that led to the steam. "Get yourself some flea powder," he called over his shoulder.

"This place is disgusting," Sergei mumbled as he took off his trousers. "I wish I were back home."

"What's that?" said an elderly man who had just entered. He looked skinny all over except for his belly, round as an onion, and he had dark age spots on his face and neck.

Sergei looked up at him. "Do you know where there are jobs in Petersburg?"

The man's face broke into a wide grin. "Yes, you're in Petersburg, best city in Russia, it is!"

Sergei shook his head and stepped into the steam bath.

上海

Sergei, still wet from his bath, bolted into his room when he saw the door ajar. He frantically rummaged through his sack to get his money pouch, but it had vanished. All his money—except for a handful of kopecks in the pocket of his trousers—was gone. On his hands and knees, Sergei scoured the floor, hoping that it had fallen out. Nothing. He threw his sack across the tiny room and ran downstairs.

"Did you leave your door open?" asked the man at the hostel counter. He wasn't the one Sergei had seen the previous night, though he looked just as mean, with jagged scars criss-crossing his face.

"Of course not," said Sergei. But as soon as the words left his lips he realized that, in his haste to get away from the rat droppings, he had.

"You sure?"

Sergei swallowed. "I think so."

The man wiped his brow with the back of his hand. "Nothing I can do."

"Can't you ask people in the rooms near mine if they saw anything?"

The man leaned forward, on his elbows. "People here don't see or hear anything."

"What?"

The man consulted the hotel register. "Guess this'll be your last night?"

Sergei nodded grimly and left.

上海

"You can try the docks," said the fruit vendor, handing Sergei an orange. "Workers from the villages come here in the summer."

Sergei handed the vendor one of his few kopecks and thanked him. With his thumb, he peeled the skin from the orange and broke off a piece. The juice spurted into his dry mouth. He ate the orange slowly and walked along the Nevsky Prospekt toward the Neva River. A troika came up from behind, the three horses trotting at a good pace. The bearded coachman sat tall and proud, his peacock-feathered hat ruffling in the wind.

The cloudy, gloomy day threatened rain. Sergei passed two men dressed in blue kaftans and caps, who he guessed were merchants from abroad. They set up a backgammon game on the underside of an empty crate. A second-hand bookshop reminded him of Rachel again.

As Sergei came to the lower end of Nevsky Prospekt, he saw churches of various denominations, colorful wood houses, sprawling warehouses, and a monastery. At the very end lay the river where women knelt on a raft, washing clothes.

About a hundred feet to his right, a large group of men worked on a wooden pontoon bridge. One kneeling worker, his face and arms covered in freckles, replaced worn-out boards on the bridge.

"Can you tell me if there's work to be had?" Sergei bent down to the man's level.

He glanced at Sergei and then went back to nailing a board in place. "You have to talk to the commandant." He tilted his head toward the middle of the bridge.

Sergei looked for the commandant amongst the men working further along the structure. He stood and slowly made his way along the bridge, held in place by pontoons moored to anchors. Every few feet a worker replaced boards that had been worn to dust by carriages.

The commandant, a thick-waisted man with a sharp voice that stung the air as he gave orders, looked at Sergei as if he were a nuisance.

"I'm looking for work," Sergei said.

The commandant snorted. "You're about two months late. These men have been working on this bridge since the ice started to break in April."

Sergei's face turned red with embarrassment. He nodded and started back to the end of the bridge.

"Hey, you—"

Sergei jerked his head left, in the direction of the robust voice, which came from a blotchy-faced boy who looked to be sixteen or seventeen years old. He lay on his stomach, his head and arms hanging over the edge of the bridge.

"The only places hiring now are the metalwork factories," said the boy. "Everywhere else—" He gestured with his hand toward the docks lining the water. "Is full."

"Factories?"

The boy smiled. "Factory work's not so bad. They pay regularly and it's year-round, not seasonal like this. I'd take it myself, only I have to go back to my father's farm when the work here is finished."

Sergei reached into his pocket, cupped his hand around the kopecks that would likely be gone by the morning, and realized he had no choice. He got directions from the boy and went in search of a trolley that would take him south for seven miles, to the chimney-laden part of town where factories puffed out smoke night and day.

上海

Sergei turned the releasing screw clockwise until it felt secure. Then he turned it the other way until it loosened. He had a trial position at the Putilov factory in the west end of Petersburg testing parts of coupling mechanisms, which connected trains. It was his third day and he had no idea if he would get the job, or how much it paid. They were evaluating his work. If he didn't get hired he wouldn't be paid for the twenty hours he'd already worked.

The foreman, a gaunt man with prominent cheekbones and sharp ears that jutted out from his head, peered at him closely, his hand on his pocket watch, as if tracking the time it took Sergei to test each component. Heat rushed to Sergei's head, a dizzy sensation that weakened his knees. The factory swarmed with men just inches from each other and there were no windows; it was difficult to breathe without gagging on the viscous air.

All day, the metallic sound of turners' lathes producing screw threads collided with the swishing hum of conveyer belts and the squeal of the circular saw, creating a constant, ear-splitting thunder. Sergei waited for his light-headedness to pass, then continued testing the parts of coupling mechanisms. He counted the minutes until the wearisome day ended.

"You're doing well," said the beefy metal fitter who worked beside Sergei. "Much better than the gray devil here last week."

Sergei nodded without stopping. He had already figured out that all the peasants were scorned. And he could see how their simple appearance gave them away—their shaggy long hair and beards, their faces etched with deep lines and dirt, and their torn and faded clothing.

A long, shrill whistle announced the end of the working day. Sergei exhaled through his nose and glanced at the foreman, speaking to a boy who looked to be eleven or twelve. The boy moved away from the foreman and approached Sergei.

"You're wanted in the office," the boy said, in a high-pitched voice.

Sergei trudged through the immense building that echoed with the sound of men's voices. All of the machines had been shut off, leaving an eerie, dull hush in the air.

About a dozen men had lined up at the office door. Sergei looked down at himself and realized he appeared as scruffy as them in his worn shirt, stained with black dirt, and his trousers wrinkled and torn at the bottom of the right leg.

The clerk wordlessly handed him a card with a number—612—along with employment papers. He told Sergei to go to the entry office at the end of the corridor.

"Have you ever worked in a factory before?" asked the man sitting behind a desk in the entry office.

"No." Sergei shook his head.

The man wrote something on a separate sheet of paper and brusquely told Sergei to proceed to the doctor's office in the next room for an exam.

A number of boys and men were waiting to see the doctor. A stodgy nurse appeared, told them to come into the examining room as a group, and instructed the men to remove their clothing. Sergei hesitated, uncomfortable with undressing in front of a woman. She looked at them blankly, as if she didn't see them at all.

The doctor, a small man with a nervous twitch in his nose, went down the line, examining one person at a time. He took their chest measurements, checked their eyesight and hearing, and gave each man a color test. Sergei pressed his teeth together when the doctor stood in front of him, and tried to think of something else as the doctor probed his body. But the doctor's hands were cold and rough, making it impossible for Sergei to focus on anything but his current discomfort.

With his employment paper marked "healthy" from the doctor, Sergei returned to the entry office and exchanged his paper for an identity tag.

"This is the most important tag you'll ever have," said the clerk gruffly. "It allows you to come into the factory to work. There's a fine of fifty kopecks for losing it, twenty kopecks for leaving it at home, and one ruble for leaving it behind in the factory."

Sergei ran his finger over his number.

"You work seven to seven, Monday to Friday, and seven to six on Saturdays," the clerk continued. "Your wage is sixty kopecks a day. Will you need housing?"

"Yes," said Sergei.

The clerk flipped through some papers. "You are assigned to bed thirty-nine in the barracks. Three hundred kopecks a week will be removed from your wages to pay for your bed and meals in the canteen."

"What? How much?"

"Three hundred," said the clerk.

"But that leaves me with just sixty kopecks after working seventy-one hours a week!"

The clerk replied. "Take it or leave it."

Sergei thought about how hard it had been to find this job. He recalled his little sister's trusting face. Natalya and his mother had so much faith in him. With his tag clenched in his hand, he made his way out of the factory, stopping briefly at the gates to be frisked for stolen tools.

Sergei followed the procession of men moving in the direction of the barracks. Hundreds walked slowly along the dirt road, past a row of small shacks built for married workers with higher designations than Sergei: master metalworkers, master drillers, master joiners. As they approached a tavern on the right side of the road, a group of men broke away from the procession, funneling into the tavern. More left to enter the beer hall beside the tavern.

When he reached the barracks, Sergei was only one of about twenty who had not succumbed to the lure of the tavern. He opened a wooden door and found himself in a low-roofed building with rows of identical metal cots. His jaw dropped as he took in the surroundings: the washed clothing hung on ropes strewn from rafters; the filthy, rudimentary table cluttered with dirty plates and bowls; the plain rectangular pillars that supported the wooden roof; and the faint light that spurted through the two square windows. Though he stood only a few miles from the center of Petersburg, where lavish buildings and statues adorned streets and gardens, he felt as if he were in a completely different place.

The potent stench of alcohol, horseradish, and body odor hovered in the air as Sergei made his way to bed thirty-nine. A couple of men sat on their cots lighting cigarettes and removing their boots. Sergei dropped onto his cot, feeling lonely and superfluous, like a fourth horse harnessed to a troika.

上海

Inside the factory, a scream caused Sergei to jump and drop the releasing screw on the ground. Another yelp of pain erupted from the corner of the factory on Sergei's right, bringing workers to a standstill. Machines whirred to a stop and the foreman walked briskly in the direction of the sound, now a jaw-clenching groan of agony.

Men gathered around the injured man. Cries of anguish

and shouts summoned the doctor, who appeared and knelt over the writhing worker.

"Just another injury," said Lev, the pockmarked man who worked near Sergei. Lev stroked his nut-brown mustache and gave Sergei a wry smile, revealing a significant gap between his front teeth. "Better get used to it." He spat on the ground, a couple of inches from Sergei's feet.

"How long have you worked here?" asked Sergei, keeping one eye on the growing chaos surrounding the injured man.

"Almost five years, since I was about your age."

Sergei choked on his own phlegm. He had assumed Lev to be at least thirty from the deep lines etched around his mouth, the heavy bags under his eyes, and his hunched-over posture—but Lev would only be twenty-one.

The doctor had the injured man carried away and the crowd thinned. The foreman walked back to his station behind Sergei, shaking his head.

"Damn, Noskov," he said as he neared Sergei and Lev. "Got his hand torn off, but left his identity tag at home. Ten years on the job. You'd think he'd know better. Damn."

"Can't somebody go and get it for him?" asked Sergei.

"Wouldn't make a difference." Lev grimaced. "No identity tag at the factory means he's not officially here, so he can't get any compensation for his hand."

"But that's not right," said Sergei. "He has lost his hand working here. He deserves something."

"Keep your voice down," instructed the foreman.

Lev peered around the factory. "The last worker who protested against the unfairness ended up being shipped off to Siberia."

"What?" Sergei looked at Lev and then at the foreman.

The foreman moved closer to Sergei until they stood chest to chest. "Don't complain," he snarled.

Sergei, smelling tobacco on the foreman's breath, met his unwavering gaze. He nodded gravely and turned back to his work. Sergei did not speak for the rest of his shift.

上海

"You seemed pretty upset about Noskov."

Sergei marched away from the gates of the plant, twisted his head and saw Lev beside him, a cigarette dangling from the side of his mouth.

"Did you know him?" asked Lev.

Sergei shook his head.

"It happens. People get hurt all the time here."

Sergei's chest burned as he recalled Noskov crying out in pain. "I know there will be accidents, but the whole business about identity tags is wrong."

Lev shrugged and took the cigarette out of his mouth. "Listen, openly objecting will lead to exile in Siberia."

Sergei stopped walking and faced Lev. "I thought things would be different, here." He resumed walking, his feet shuffling along lethargically as they passed rowdy taverns and beer halls.

"Come with me." Lev grabbed Sergei's shoulder and pulled him roughly into the Golden Bird Tavern, through a doorway barely wide enough for one man to pass.

Sergei had once been a regular in Kishinev taverns, but only to extract his drunken father and bring him home. Still, as his vision grew accustomed to the dusky light, he saw that this tavern looked much cruder than any he'd seen before, with its gray, sooty walls, barrels for chairs, and an oily factory smell that made his nostrils itch.

Sergei followed Lev to a small, round table in the far corner and sat on the edge of a barrel. The ring of the orchestrion machine saturated the air with cheap imitation of real music.

Lev ordered two ashberry brandies and rested his calloused elbows on the table. Sergei opened his mouth to tell Lev that he didn't drink, that he'd seen how alcohol could destroy a man—his father for example. But the words got stuck in his throat. Lots of men drank but didn't lose control like his father, Sergei reasoned. He wanted to be a better person than his father, stronger, more reliable, honest. Sober.

When their brandies arrived, Lev tilted his head back and downed the alcohol in one gulp. Sergei lifted his glass to his lips and took a small sip. The strong, bitter brandy seared his throat. Sergei took another, bigger sip and his face and neck warmed.

Lev leaned forward. "If you're so upset about the way they treat us in factories, there's a group you might want to join." He motioned for another two brandies. "But you can't repeat what I'm about to tell you." His eyes swept the room and he lowered his voice. "Men have been sentenced to hard labor, exile, even killed for being involved."

Sergei fixed his gaze on Lev.

Lev turned his head right, then left before continuing. "It's the Party of Socialist Revolutionaries. This is an organization that works in support of the Russian working people, like us in the factory, who suffer from low wages and unsafe working conditions. The party organizes strikes at factories, where all the workers refuse to work and demonstrate together outside the factory buildings. The Party's goal is to force the government to make changes that will improve all our lives."

"What?"

"The Party—"

"I heard you. Are you a member?"

"For about seven months now."

"But people have been killed striking—"

"Accidentally, when the government has interfered with our strikes."

"Don't you think it's a bit crazy, risking your life like that?"

Lev drained his brandy. "You've been on the job three weeks now?"

"Four." Sergei scratched his head nervously.

"And how many accidents have you seen?"

"Maybe three or four."

Lev slid his glass across the table for the server to fill again. He waited until she finished pouring before continuing.

"That's an accident once a week, at least. We work so many damn hours that we're often half asleep on the job. It's only a matter of time before you or I make a mistake."

Sergei's shoulders heaved up and down. "You could be right. But I can't join a dangerous party that rebels against the government."

Lev sat back, crossed his arms, and gave Sergei a disappointed look. "Let me know when you change your mind."

"I won't. I can't."

"We'll see."

5

"Look, Rachel!" Menahem pointed to the left of the shores of Vladivostok. The city receded quickly as the steamship moved through Golden Horn Bay for five miles into the Sea of Japan. From there, they'd enter the East China Sea for two miles, ending up on the Pacific Ocean, which would carry them almost nine hundred miles to Shanghai, China. They stood on the crowded steerage deck with Shprintze and Isaac. Rachel's mother and Nucia rested below in their bunks.

Rachel followed Menahem's hand and saw two tall, reddish-brown rocks jutting out from the water, the Little Verkhovsky Islands.

"They look like two triangles," said Rachel. "It's amazing how similar they are, as if hand-carved."

"I wish Sergei could see this," said Menahem.

"Someday he will," said Rachel. She stared at the unusual rock formation, as unexpected as a rainbow, until it became just a speck in the navy blue water and let the wind chill her face.

"I could stay here forever," said Menahem, clutching the railing with both hands and thrusting his face into the wind.

Rachel tousled the boy's hair, and returned her gaze to the surprisingly smooth water surrounding them. She wished she could keep this feeling of serenity with her always.

But soon the conditions changed. As the ship moved farther from land, deeper into the Sea of Japan, the water grew choppy and the wind became stronger. Rachel's stomach churned and her legs wobbled as the ship heaved from side to side. Menahem suddenly leaned over the railing and retched into the sea. His face grew pale and his eyeballs rolled up. Seeing Menahem throwing up turned Rachel's stomach inside out. She lunged forward and vomited until there was nothing left inside.

"Are you all right?" asked Shprintze when Rachel finished and collapsed into a heap on the deck.

Rachel shook her head: it seemed like an enormous effort to move. She tried to stay as still as possible to keep her insides from rebelling against the rolling motion.

Menahem, still leaning against the rail, turned toward Rachel. "I think I feel better. I want to see Mother Ita."

"I'll take you," said Shprintze, reaching out for Menahem's hand.

"I'll go too," croaked Rachel. "Maybe it will be calmer for my stomach inside." She stood unsteadily and grasped Isaac's outstretched arm.

The minute she stepped into the underbelly of the ship, Rachel knew she'd made a mistake. The smell of body odor and fish soup made her stomach act up again. She scrambled over the steps and ran to the side of the ship. But nothing came out of her mouth.

She turned her face into the wind, letting the blustery air cleanse her head and soothe her stomach. Then, she slunk down onto her bottom and leaned against the railing. The sun had started to set over the sea, casting a purplish-pink haze at the horizon, where the light blue sky met the indigo-blue water. The cool air numbed her skin until she became too cold to stay outside. Once again, she made her way down the stairs to the steerage section. Rachel lay down on the bunk she shared with Menahem but, within minutes, her stomach revolted again. With one hand clutching her abdomen, she ran up the stairs and hung her head over the edge of the ship.

When Rachel's stomach pains finally subsided, she sat down on the deck. Her thoughts returned to Kishinev, when she'd been about eight years old and had fallen ill for days. Her father had stayed up with her all night while her throat burned with pain. He'd cooled her brow with a wet cloth and made tea with honey to soothe her throat. He'd told her stories, fairy tales about mesmerizing people like Vasilissa, a beautiful girl who outwitted her evil stepmother. And Princess Solima, so melancholy, her father decided she should marry and see other places. But she said she would only marry a man who did not think that he was the most important person in the world. Princess Solima's father imprisoned her in his fortress in the sea. Eventually, a poor shepherd boy who tried to save an ox from a monstrous bird, found himself atop a tower in the sea. There, he saw the princess and they fell in love. They returned to the king's palace and the princess told her father that her husband was a prince among men, a man without riches, who came from the people and would understand their needs and know how to rule them.

Now Rachel imagined herself as Princess Solima and Sergei as the shepherd boy. She pictured the two of them, holding hands, on a tower rising up from the sea. But the sea grew rough and the tower began to sway back and forth, back and forth, getting closer to the turbulent water until it plunged in, vanishing forever.

上海

On their second day at sea, Rachel's mother began coughing violently. Unable to sleep, she'd joined Rachel on the deck early in the morning. During a particularly violent fit, Rachel helplessly watched her mother as the coughs overtook her weakened body. Her skin had turned gray, almost translucent, and her lips looked dry and chapped.

"What's that on your—" Rachel stared at her mother's hand, which had covered her mouth during the fit, and saw bright red smudges. "Blood, it's blood."

Her mother gazed down at her hand and looked up at Rachel with a confused expression. Rachel sensed someone watching them. She turned and saw passengers, all with fearful expressions, backing away from them. *What if we're thrown off the ship now?*

"You have to see a doctor," said Rachel, biting her lip. She waited for her mother to argue, but she bowed her head meekly and accepted this news without a fight.

"I should have stayed in Russia," Ita said. "I am causing you nothing but trouble."

"We never could have left without you," said Rachel. "You'll get better soon, when you have a warm place to sleep and good food."

Ita began to cough again. Rachel held her tight and they went in search of the doctor.

上海

"It's hard to be certain, but I'd say it's consumption," said Dr. Frieden, a bushy-haired man with fleshy cheeks. Kneeling, he examined Ita right on the deck, peering into her throat, feeling the glands on her neck, and listening to her cough. He had covered his own mouth with a cloth.

"Can you—" Rachel gulped. "Can you make her better?"

The doctor slowly got to his feet and shook his head. "I'm sorry."

These two words hung awkwardly between Rachel and the doctor for a moment. She looked at her mother, lying on her side, her hipbones protruding sharply under her skin.

"But there's a chance?" she said.

"Maybe, if I'm wrong. But she's in bad shape. Your mother will have to be quarantined with other sick passengers."

"Where?" asked Rachel, in tears.

"There's a place on the other side of the ship, away from the rest of us."

"No, she can stay on the deck with me," Rachel protested. "I'll take care of her. And I'll make sure nobody comes near us."

"That's not possible," said the doctor vaguely. He motioned to two members of the ship's crew and explained that he needed help moving a woman to the quarantine area.

The two young men positioned themselves at her mother's head and feet, lifting her as if she were a small child.

"I want to come too, to see where she'll be," said Rachel.

"The area is off-limits," the doctor replied. "I'm surprised nobody else in your family has been affected," the doctor continued. "To be on the safe side, I'd like to give you all a short examination." He told Rachel to gather her family quickly.

Rachel watched her mother being carried away and clenched her teeth. *Mother wouldn't be this ill if we hadn't had to make the long and difficult journey from Kishinev*, she fumed. *Her poor health is a terrible price to pay for our getaway.*

上海

After five days at sea, the ship finally docked in Shanghai. A heavy rain came down in sheets, pummeling the ship without stopping. Rachel's stomach felt as if it had been broken into hundreds of pieces by then. As she waited in the long line to go up the stairs, the foul stink of garbage and sewage seeped through the ship's hull. Rachel grimaced and pinched her nose with her hand.

"Phew," said Menahem. "What a horrible smell!"

"Hold your nose," Rachel told him. She glanced over her shoulder and winced when she saw Shprintze's face contorted with disgust.

The rain continued, increasing its intensity as they moved up in the line—as if it was anxious to greet them, or to warn them away.

From somewhere ahead of Rachel, a baby cried. Nucia, standing beside Rachel, had a bland look on her face, as if she were unaffected by the smells and the noise. Since their mother had been quarantined, Nucia had retreated into herself, speaking flatly and gazing vacantly into the distance.

"Will Mother Ita come back now?" asked Menahem.

Panic flickered across Rachel's face. "I hope so."

"I'm sure she misses you," added Shprintze. She and Isaac stood behind Rachel.

"Do you think her cough is better?" said Menahem.

"I hope so," Rachel repeated.

"What if she's not better?" pressed Menahem.

"Stop asking so many questions."

Menahem's head dropped forward.

Rachel took his hand and held it tight. She thought about promising him that everything would be fine. But that would have been a lie.

6

Though the rain had stopped, the humidity sheathed Rachel like a second clammy skin as she made her way up to the deck. A diminutive woman in a black sarafan, caked with grime, cradled a baby in one arm and held onto a small child with the other. Rachel examined her own long brown cotton skirt: stains blotted the fabric and the frayed hem hung limply around her ankles. Her blouse, ripped under the arms, stuck to her moist, unwashed skin. *I look like a beggar.* She straightened her spine and held her head high. *If I must look like a beggar, than at least I will walk proudly.*

When Rachel arrived on the deck, she peered down the ship to see if her mother stood nearby. No sign of her or any other ill passengers. She scanned the muddy water with pieces of rubbish floating on top. As she stepped off the ship onto the dock, the stench of dead fish engulfed her.

"Ech," said Rachel. "This smell…it's horrible!"

"Maybe it will smell better when we're far from the water," said Shprintze.

"I doubt it," said Rachel. She walked along the dock, staring at the Chinese crowd that gathered around them. Their gaping stares made Rachel uneasy. She put her arm around Menahem as they neared the throng of people. They were immediately surrounded on all sides, their skin rubbing against their fellow passengers, as well as the Chinese. As they moved with the crowd to the reception station, a large white building with an octagonal tower protruding from the roof, strange, clipped sounds arose from the people of Shanghai.

"What are they saying?" asked Menahem.

"I don't know their language." Rachel's stomach twisted with anxiety. "Just stay with us. Whatever you do, don't wander away."

Menahem wrapped his arm tightly around Rachel's waist.

"Are you sure we don't need visas to enter Shanghai?" asked Nucia, after they had been standing in a line that led to a white building for almost an hour.

"Yes, I'm sure," said Rachel. "But they still have to keep track of the people coming here."

"We must all be patient," added Shprintze. "Our turn will come."

As they waited, a woman with a long neck and flaxen hair, the color of her skin, made her way through the line. She spoke excitedly with her hands as well as her mouth. She wore a red-and-black Chinese robe that went down to her feet. Her hair had been pulled back severely and around her neck hung a chain with a gold cross.

"I'm with the China Inland Mission," she said in Russian, addressing Nucia, touching her shoulder gently as she spoke. "Through God's grace and power, we're working to glorify Jesus in Shanghai."

Nucia looked blankly at the woman.

Rachel and Shprintze exchanged worried glances. "What's wrong, Rachel?" asked Menahem.

Rachel ran her tongue over her upper lip. Did this woman want them to join her Christian mission? Would she be angry if she discovered they were Jewish?

"We can't talk now," said Isaac. He nodded at the missionary woman.

"Are you mad at that lady?" Menahem squinted up at Isaac.

"Just a little, but don't worry. Everything is fine."

"Do you think we were brought here to be converted to Christianity?" whispered Nucia to Rachel.

Rachel considered her sister's words. "I don't know. But what will they do to us if we don't convert?"

Nucia shook her head.

Rachel gazed back at the choppy sea and worried whether they would find themselves back on the water sooner than they expected, heading back toward Russia and away from America.

上海

Rachel lifted her braids from her sweaty neck when she walked into the white building. It had been hours since they'd disembarked from the ship. A Chinese woman sitting behind a shiny black table gestured with her hand for Rachel to come see her. The woman had glossy black hair pulled into a tight bun and smooth amber skin. Rachel couldn't stop staring at her almond-shaped eyes.

The woman pushed a sheet of paper to the edge of the table and handed Rachel a quill pen. The paper, written in Russian, asked for the name of her hometown, her age, occupation, and the names of family members traveling with her.

"My mother was quarantined on the ship," Rachel said in Russian, her tone becoming more urgent as she spoke. "Ita Paskar is her name. When can I see her?"

The woman gave Rachel a hard look as she flipped through some pages in front of her. "Ita Paskar," she mumbled. Though she spoke in Russian, her pronunciation sounded odd, choppy, and stilted. She ran her finger along the writing on a page and stopped. "I'm afraid not. She will remain in quarantine here, and if she does not improve, she'll be sent back to Russia."

"But you can't do that. We have no family left there. You can't send her back!"

The woman dropped the papers and folded her hands together. "I don't make the rules." She looked at Rachel, waiting for her to fill out the required forms.

Rachel began to write; her hand trembled. Some of her words were illegible, but she didn't care. *What if I get sick, or Nucia, or Menahem? Will they send us back, too?*

The woman called out to someone in Chinese. A male voice answered and the two began to shout back and forth across the room. A nurse, dressed in white, appeared. Rachel followed the nurse to the corner of the room, blocked off for privacy with muslin curtains.

"A doctor on the ship already examined everyone in my family," protested Rachel.

"You must still be inspected here," said the nurse. She instructed Rachel to open her mouth. After peering into her throat, the nurse pressed against Rachel's neck with rough fingers. She used a stethoscope to check Rachel's heart and then probed every inch of her skin, including her scalp.

"What are you looking for?" asked Rachel.

"Bumps, bruises, cuts, scars, lice," said the nurse matter-of-factly. "To see if you have any history of disease."

Rachel gritted her teeth and stood stiffly until the nurse pronounced her healthy. She signed a piece of paper and handed it to Rachel.

"Give this to the woman sitting across from here," said the nurse.

Rachel plodded out of the makeshift curtained room and gave Nucia, next to be examined, a frustrated look. The woman across from the nurse's station took the paper from her and dipped a brush into a pot of ink. Rachel watched, intrigued, as the woman's hands moved gracefully, swiftly creating a delicate pattern of brush strokes that looked more like art than written language.

The woman finished, handed the paper back to Rachel, and pointed to her right, at a line with other families on the far side of the room. "What am I waiting for now?"

The woman shrugged, as if she didn't understand what Rachel had asked. With an impatient sigh, Rachel moved over to the line, which spanned thirty feet. Shprintze and Isaac stood in front of Rachel with glum expressions.

"Mother's not coming with us, is she?" said Nucia, when she joined Rachel.

"If she doesn't get better, they're going to send her back," Rachel said in a monotone voice.

"Send her back?"

"Send who back?" demanded Menahem, who had just arrived in the line.

"Mother Ita," said Rachel. "If she doesn't get better."

"To Russia?" asked Menahem.

"Only if her cough doesn't improve." Nucia put her hand on his back.

Rachel, her eyes brimming with tears, held Menahem tightly to her chest until he complained that he couldn't breathe.

A wiry Chinese man appeared, spreading his hands wide and moving them back together again. He repeated this as he progressed through the crowd, leaving a lot of puzzled faces in his wake.

"I think he wants us to move against the wall," said Isaac.

Rachel followed Isaac's gaze to people on the other side of the room, shuffling back to the wall. The Chinese man looked at them and smiled. Rachel, along with the rest of the people on her side, stepped back until they touched the wall. Soon, every inch of the room was covered with passengers.

After the room had been cleared, men entered, carrying tables and chairs. Within minutes, the room had been set up to serve a meal.

"I don't feel very well," said Menahem, once they'd taken seats in the middle of the room.

Rachel studied Menahem's face. His cheekbones jutted out against his skin and yellowish-gray circles underlined his eyes.

"I feel sick—" Menahem flung his hands over his mouth. He fell off his chair and retched.

"Oh no!" cried Rachel. She bent down and put her hand over his heaving shoulders. A woman sitting next to Menahem, with a baby in her arms, leapt out of her chair and hurried to get away from Menahem.

"I'll ask for something to clean it up," said Nucia in a nasal tone as her fingers squeezed her nostrils shut. She walked back to the glossy-haired woman and moved her hand in circles, to give the impression of scrubbing. The woman handed her a beige cloth, which Nucia used to wipe up the vomit.

"I'm sure he's just nervous, being in a strange country," said Isaac, helping Nucia clean the mess with another cloth.

Menahem, his face as white as the sails on their ship, sat cross-legged on the ground, wiping tears from his face. Shprintze pulled a rag out of her pouch, cleaned Menahem's face, and gave him a motherly embrace. Rachel tried to smile, pushing away her feelings of inadequacy when it came to caring for Menahem. She felt grateful for finding such a loyal and kind friend as Shprintze.

上海

The waiting room had grown loud with voices and the air had become gritty with so many unwashed bodies in one place. Rachel's family, along with Shprintze and Isaac, sat at a long table with a dozen other people, waiting for food, which was being handed out by several Chinese women. Rachel's forehead creased when she received a porcelain bowl of white, fluffy food, along with a cup of tea and two identical sticks.

"It looks like a cloud in a bowl," said Menahem. It had been more than two hours since he'd been sick and color had returned to his face, along with his endearing grin.

Rachel sniffed her food, taking in the rising steam and faint floral scent.

"What do we eat this with?" Nucia asked.

Rachel and Menahem picked up the sticks and examined them. "Do we scoop the food?" Rachel asked.

Menahem tried to use the sticks as a scoop, but the white grains fell off. He shrugged his shoulders, dropped the sticks back onto the table and used his fingers. Rachel watched him for a second and followed his example. A few minutes later, they were all eating with their fingers.

"It's very spicy," said Shprintze.

Rachel moved the food around in her mouth and swallowed. "It feels like seeds in my mouth."

Menahem looked into his almost-empty bowl. "I think it looks like white mouse droppings."

"Menahem!" Nucia froze, with her hand in her bowl.

Isaac started to laugh. A loud, hearty laugh.

Shprintze joined in, almost dropping her bowl as she chortled, sending Menahem into a giggling fit.

Shortly after the bowls were taken away, Chinese men motioned for everyone to stand. They began pushing the tables back against the walls.

"Are we allowed to go into the city of Shanghai now?" Rachel asked in Russian of one man with a shiny bald head and whiskers.

He looked at her with an uncomprehending expression and went back to shifting tables. Rachel shrugged her shoulders at Nucia and watched the other passengers who milled about in groups. Some men paced back and forth, talking in low, urgent voices. Other women tried to calm fussy babies and sad-looking children who looked older than their years. The musty air weighed Rachel down. She worried she'd fall asleep standing up.

Three women came in with baskets containing rolled-up blankets. Their shiny black hair was pulled into sleek buns and they wore long skirts and buttoned shirts. The women handed one thin blanket to each person and gestured to the floor.

"Do we have to sleep here?" asked Menahem.

"I think so," said Rachel. She unrolled her blanket and spread it on the floor.

Menahem set his blanket beside Rachel's. Nucia put hers on the other side of Menahem, so that he could sleep between the two sisters. Shprintze and Isaac lay across from them.

"I don't know why they even bothered with these blankets," muttered Rachel. "The floor's still hard as ice." She rolled onto her left side, then rolled over to her right side.

"I wish someone would explain what's going on," said Nucia.

"I think we're in quarantine," said Rachel.

"But we're not sick," said Menahem.

Rachel explained how they were being isolated from the Shanghai people, to make sure they didn't bring in any diseases. As she spoke, Rachel pictured her mother lying by herself, in a room full of ill strangers.

"I wish Mother were here," whispered Nucia to Rachel.

"Me, too."

"She's going to get better, isn't she?" asked Menahem.

"Mother's a strong woman," said Rachel. She recalled the many times her mother had been mad at her for misbehaving, for not doing what she'd been asked to do, and wished she could hear her mother's voice now, even if it meant being scolded.

上海

During two monotonous days in quarantine, the nuns tried to convince the Jewish refugees to convert to Christianity.

"We haven't come all this way only to give up our faith and our heritage," said Rachel, when a particularly assertive nun pressed her one evening after supper. "If we'd stayed in Russia and converted, people would have left us alone. We'd be accepted as gentiles. Instead we chose to leave in order to keep our faith." The nun, coolly resigned, left for the next table without another word to Rachel.

Before being released from quarantine, the Russian Jews were given basic information about living in Shanghai—to convert their rubles and kopecks into the local currency: *yuan, jiao,* and *fen.* They were also told to prepare for the rainy season and possibly typhoons.

"Remember to stay in the International Settlement," said a stubby Russian nurse. She told people to find a hostel in Shanghai's International Settlement, in the north end of the city. She explained that this region was a combination of two distinct areas with its own police force and municipal council— the American Concession on the east side of the Huangpu River and the British Concession on the west side. A separate French Concession could be found south of the British Concession.

"Russians will go to the British Concession," she instructed, opening the door to the outside world.

"Before we go," said Rachel, "I want to find the quarantined passengers."

"Why?" asked the nurse.

"My mother is there," said Rachel.

"You cannot see her."

"I need to. I don't want her to think we've forgotten about her."

The woman shook her head vehemently.

Rachel searched the woman's obstinate face for a hint of empathy, but saw none. "Please, just for a moment."

The woman's tight lips did not move.

Discouraged but not defeated, Rachel joined her sister and Menahem, vowing silently to keep trying to find her mother.

7

Shanghai hit Rachel like a storm with its myriad of people, animals, food, and smells. Colorful banners hung over the street as far as Rachel could see, with distinctive symbols that looked like brush strokes. The sidewalks and streets swarmed with people walking in both directions. Rachel's shoulder was jostled as she followed Isaac and Shprintze down Stechuen Road. As they continued, short, wiry Chinese men worked like horses, pulling passengers in two-wheeled carts called rickshaws. They filled the muddy road, moving briskly. One pulled up behind Shprintze, and the little man pointed at his cart and then at her. Shprintze shook her head and the man continued on.

"That's dreadful," said Rachel, still watching the man with the cart. "A person doing an animal's job."

"Terrible," agreed Shprintze, wrinkling her nose.

"Look at their funny hats," said Menahem, staring at an

assortment of men, who wore yellow straw hats with narrow brims.

"Stop staring," said Nucia sternly. She grabbed his hand and tugged him along with her.

Shprintze bent down and whispered to Menahem: "I think the hats look funny, too."

Menahem giggled, saw Nucia's grim expression, and slapped his hand over his mouth.

"It's odd, being surrounded by people so completely different from us," said Rachel. She dropped back to walk beside Shprintze, her eyes moving from side to side as she took in her surroundings.

A couple of Chinese men yelled and gestured wildly with their hands. As Rachel and Shprintze walked past them, they stopped talking and watched the girls intently.

"They could be saying all kinds of things about us and we'd never know," said Rachel, after they'd passed the men.

"They could be thinking the same about us," said Shprintze.

"True," agreed Rachel. All of a sudden she felt overwhelmed by the distance they'd traveled. For the first time in her life, she was in a different unknown country. She worried that her mother had become desperately ill and could no longer guide them. Their funds were dwindling, and Rachel felt the enormous responsibility toward Menahem, since Sergei had placed him in her hands. She twisted her braid around her fingers and bit down on her bottom lip.

They crossed a greenish-brown river that rose dangerously high, sloshing over the rickety bridge, soaking their feet. Barges and rafts cluttered the water. Bamboo roofs over unusual slipper-shaped boats provided shade for the fishermen on board.

"We turn right here," said Isaac, when they came to Nanking Road. Up ahead, others from the ship plodded in the direction of the British Concession.

Rachel swatted the dense cloud of flies that had followed her from the ship. The flies buzzing around her head seemed to multiply by the minute. Her feet felt slimy, and the gray clouds overhead swelled and threatened rain.

Nanking Road, a broad avenue, was lined with four-storey buildings with signs written in many languages, other than Chinese. English, German, Russian, and Jewish shops, restaurants and hotels stood on both sides of the street.

"I don't feel like I'm in China," said Rachel. "The buildings look completely different from the ones we saw at the wharf."

"And there are hardly any Chinese people here," added Shprintze. "Only Chinese men pulling carts."

When they found a Russian bank, they entered to change their money. Inside, it looked much like a Kishinev bank, only smaller and with fewer employees. The front window overlooked the street, and a counter, the width of the bank, divided the public from the staff. At the back, men sat at desks, oblivious to the business taking place at the front.

Isaac went first, approaching the young man at the counter, getting Chinese coins in return for rubles and kopecks. Nucia and Rachel followed, with Nucia carefully emptying their pouch and placing a small amount of money on the counter.

"That's all we have?" asked Rachel. She picked up one of the few rubles and put it back down.

Nucia turned the pouch inside out. Rachel groaned.

The man began counting their money, his hands moving

the coins so swiftly that Rachel feared he'd lose count. He opened a drawer beneath the counter and counted out the appropriate sum in Chinese currency. Nucia stuffed the money in the pouch and thanked him.

"Welcome to Shanghai," said the man, gawking at Nucia.

A red flush crept up Nucia's neck, onto her cheeks. "Thank you."

They headed down the street, Rachel peering in every direction, taking in the foreign languages, the indecipherable billboards and signs, and the unusual-looking people. Strangest of all were a group of olive-skinned men with dark whiskers, wearing turbans on their heads and white, flowing robes that fell almost to their feet. They stood in front of a posh building, the Astor House Hotel, made of stone with tall windows and a wide front door.

"*Shalom*," said one of these men in Hebrew as Rachel approached.

"Shalom," Rachel echoed faintly, wondering why this man spoke Hebrew. He looked nothing like any Jew she'd ever met.

"*Boker tov*," said another man in Hebrew. He was the oldest in the group with long, gray whiskers and deeply etched lines on his face.

Isaac, who understood Hebrew, stopped and asked the man in Hebrew where he'd come from.

"Baghdad," he replied. "We have been here in Shanghai for years."

"And you?" asked a younger man with bulging black eyeballs.

"Russia," answered Isaac.

All the Baghdad men nodded solemnly.

"We have been reading about the pogroms in Russia," said the oldest man. "You will find peace here."

"There is a fine Jewish school for the boy," added the man with the bulging eyeballs, "and plenty of work, for this settlement grows by the day."

"This is very good news," said Isaac, "but right now, we need to find a hostel that is not too expensive."

"Yes, yes," said the oldest man. He pointed to his left and said there would be a street that came off Nanking Road with a clean Jewish hostel. "Foochow Road." He bowed and moved aside to allow more room on the sidewalk for the group to pass.

Rachel hesitated; she had a chill from her soggy feet, rain had begun to fall, and the others were already striding ahead. But a question burned inside of her.

"Where do the Chinese people live?" she asked the oldest man.

"They live in the old city," he replied. "This is a small, round area hidden behind walls and gates that were built to protect them from Japanese pirates."

"Pirates?"

He chuckled. "A long time ago. You needn't worry about pirates now."

Rachel smiled. "I must join my family."

The old man nodded. Rachel began walking quickly to catch up with everyone, reaching them just as they were about to turn onto Foochow Road, a narrow, crooked road with Jewish shops on both sides. The rain, which had intensified, splattered mud at their feet and cast a gloomy mood over the street.

上海

"I suppose we should go inside and ask about rooms before we're totally drenched," said Rachel, tilting her head back to look at the squalid hostel.

Standing four storeys tall, the roofline of the narrow building appeared to sag in the middle. To the right stood a bakery with a pyramid of *challah* in the window, and on the left a candle shop. The shop windows, smudged and dirty, were uninviting, but the familiar Yiddish signs provided Rachel with a welcome relief from the onslaught of undecipherable billboards.

"Do you think this is the one he meant?" said Shprintze, casting a skeptical look at Rachel.

"I don't see any other hostel on this street," she replied.

Lightening flashed overhead, illuminating the sky. Rachel marched forward and opened the hostel door. Shprintze and Isaac followed, with Menahem and Nucia close behind. Inside, a tired-looking woman glanced up from a worn table that she'd been scrubbing.

Rachel introduced herself and explained that they were looking for rooms.

The woman dropped her cloth into a bucket and wiped her hands on her skirt. "My name's Danka Muller. How many rooms do you need?"

"Two."

Danka Muller told them that rooms cost two jiao a night, and included two meals a day. Nucia counted out enough money for one room for three nights and handed it to her. Isaac did the same for himself and Shprintze.

Rachel's mind kept working. *We'll be living in the streets before long if we don't start making money soon. We may never save enough money to go to America; we might end up living out*

80 Shelly Sanders

our days here, stuck forever between our former life and an elusive chance at a new one.

Rachel walked into the dingy, second-floor room and gulped. The distance from side to side had to be less than ten feet. Two rickety cots, like those that had been in the Kishinev hospital, were pressed against opposite walls. A wooden basin and bucket sat beside the door. A very large black bug crawled out from under the cot farthest from the door.

"Ech, that's disgusting," said Nucia, stepping back into the corridor.

"What is it?" asked Menahem, moving closer, his eyes pasted on the bug.

"A cockroach, I think," answered Rachel, reaching for the bucket. "I heard people talking about them while we were at the inspection area this morning."

Nucia sat down on the other cot and raised her feet.

Rachel lifted the bucket, turned it over, and dropped it on the bug. "There." She slid the bucket over to the open door, pushed it into the corridor, and shut the door. "I'll ask for another one."

Before Rachel had time to congratulate herself, a man's shouts erupted from behind one wall followed by a woman's cries. Rachel walked to the only window, overlooking a narrow lane at the back. The glass was opaque with grime and Rachel smelled a foul mixture of excrement and dead fish. She wiped tears from her face and stared outside; rain had begun to fall again, pounding the window like pebbles.

"Where do we all sleep, Rachel?" asked Menahem.

"You and I will share one cot and Nucia will take the other," she said with as much authority as she could manage. She sat down wearily on the edge of her cot, waited for Menahem to get comfortable beside her, and then she lay down. But she could not sleep. The outside noises rose as night fell—men shouting out in a strange, harsh language; the faint sound of music from farther away; the smattering of feet on the road beneath her room; and babies crying.

The next morning, Rachel plugged her nose and carried the bucket down the narrow staircase with one hand. When she opened the front door, the soggy morning air wet her skin, jolting her awake. She traipsed to the street, flooded with several inches of murky rainwater, and dropped the bucket down beside the others from their hostel. The putrid stench made her nostrils sting and her stomach lurch. It smelled like the inside of an outhouse.

A wagon approached, its wheels making a loud rickety sound. An old Chinese man, bent with age, pulled it and emptied toilet buckets into its back end.

With both hands over her mouth, Rachel stumbled, regained her balance, then rushed into the hostel, and slammed the door shut.

The next evening, Rachel tried to think about something good, something that would make her happy to share with Menahem. She recalled the night she'd told Sergei one of her favorite stories by the Yiddish writer Sholem Aleichem. She pictured herself sitting under the stars in Kishinev, beside Sergei, and, within seconds, the din surrounding her in the boarding house receded. Then she told the story to Menahem.

"Tevye was a dairyman with five daughters. He always bemoaned the fact that he was poor and had so many mouths to feed. But he kept his humor about the situation. 'You can't fill a stomach with words,' Tevye would say. Or 'What a shame it is we have mouths, because if we didn't we'd never grow hungry.' Or 'If you're looking to buy something, I'm afraid I'm all out of stock. Unless I can interest you in some fine hunger pangs, a week's supply of heartache, or a head full of scrambled brains.'"

Rachel smiled, remembering how Sergei had chuckled over Tevye's phrases. She furrowed her brow in concentration and went on telling the story to Menahem. "On his way home one day, he came across two women who lost their way. These women talked Tevye into driving them home with his horse and wagon, even though it was in the opposite direction of his home. When they arrived at their home, Tevye saw that they were wealthy. They shared their food with Tevye, loaded his wagon with more food for his family, and paid him a small fortune for helping them get home. Tevye imagined all the wonderful ways he could spend this unexpected money. But in the end, he and his wife decided to buy an extra milking cow so that Tevye would have more dairy products to sell to the rich Jews.

"Tevye realized that with his new, more prosperous, life-style rumors about him might start in the village. Some people might say that he'd passed out phony banknotes or made moonshine liquor. But one thing he knew for sure was that nobody would congratulate him on his good fortune. 'No, our Jews like to keep their praises to themselves, which is more than I can say about their noses,' said Tevye."

Menahem laughed at Tevye's joke about noses and begged Rachel to tell him another funny story.

"Tomorrow night," she promised, pulling him to her and squeezing him tight.

"Please, just one more," pleaded Menahem. He slipped from her grasp. "You're the best storyteller I've ever heard."

Rachel looked into his wide, earnest eyes and ruffled his hair. "This is the last one." She rummaged through her brain and began telling another tale about Tevye.

PART TWO
Fall 1903

Welcome to Shanghai! From now on, you are not a Russian, German, Austrian or Romanian anymore. You are only Jews.

—Shanghai Economic Relief Committee, *1903*

8

August 31, 1903
37 Foochow Road
Shanghai

Dear Sergei,

I am writing to you at your parents' address and I hope they will pass this letter on to you.

We are now safely out of Russia, and have settled as comfortably as possible in Shanghai, where it rains every day and is so hot, I feel as if I'm going to melt. At night, our room at the hostel feels like the inside of a stove. Yesterday, Menahem placed a spoon of butter on the front steps and it melted in seconds! Then he drank the butter, which made Nucia mad.

Mother took sick with a bad cough and is now quite

ill. She has been put in medical quarantine at a hospital and we cannot even get in to see her. I tried to visit her yesterday but the nurses wouldn't let me through the door. I wrote her a letter but am desperate to see her face and hear her voice.

Menahem and I miss you terribly. He asks about you every day and doesn't quite understand why you don't come for him as you had promised. I tell him that you must think of him, too, and that you will come when you are able.

I know that someday Menahem and I will see you again.

Stay well and write soon,
Your Rachel

P.S. I have enclosed drawings I've done of a couple of Chinese characters. Their language fascinates me, for it sounds rough to my ears, yet the written characters are so graceful.

Rachel tightened her grip on her empty basket and moved through the throng of people toward the heart of Shanghai, the Bund, at the edge of the Huangpu River with Nucia and Menahem. September had arrived and the air had finally cooled down. But the rivers overflowed from the summer rain, and the ground had become soft and muddy.

The Chinese presence grew as they came closer to the river. When they stepped onto Foochow Road, they entered another world. Bold signs written in Chinese symbols greeted them, and cluttered sidewalks overflowed with baskets of unrecognizable leaves and vegetables—flowering chives and orange-red fruit that looked like it had been dipped in sugar. Though she'd walked through this area many times since arriving in Shanghai, Rachel never tired of seeing these people who had given them a place to live outside of Russia.

Chinese women, sitting on low stools, signaled for Rachel to come and see what they were selling.

"No money," said Rachel in Russian, holding out the palms of her empty hands.

One woman creased her brow for a second, and said something to Rachel in Chinese, motioning for Rachel to come nearer as she spoke. Rachel forced a smile and turned away. *I wish we could understand each other*, she thought.

"Everyone always seems to be in such a hurry," said Nucia.

"I wonder what is so urgent," said Rachel.

"I'm hungry," said Menahem.

"You should've eaten your food at the hostel," Rachel told him.

"I didn't like it," he said.

"Then you mustn't have been very hungry," Rachel snapped. She too felt famished and her stomach had become upset after the small meal consisting of a piece of Yangei fruit so tart it stung the inside of her mouth, and the gray egg that tasted as if it was spoiled. "I'm sorry, Menahem. Let's find something to eat."

"We need to save our money," said Nucia. "There's hardly any left and I don't start work for two days."

"I won't have the strength to keep looking for a job if I don't get a decent meal soon," said Rachel. "A robin would starve on what we get at the hostel."

"Why do you have to be so difficult?" asked Nucia.

"Why do you have to be so perfect?"

"Perfect? What do you mean?"

"You never complain," said Rachel. "I know your stomach is empty. I can hear it growling."

Nucia's face grew red; she glanced down at her stomach. "Being grumpy won't fill my stomach."

"But it makes me feel better, getting angry," said Rachel. "If I try to ignore my hunger, I feel worse, as if my stomach is going to turn inside out."

Menahem looked puzzled.

Nucia chortled. "Fine. We'll get something to eat."

Rachel squeezed her sister tight. "I promise tomorrow I'll find a job."

They continued walking under a multitude of long white banners hanging motionlessly in the still air. On the sidewalk, Chinese men and women sat with their goods—silk, thread, newspapers, and food that gave off strong odors of garlic and onion as they drew closer. There were fish crammed into barrels, live frogs and snakes in cages, and chickens squawking fitfully, as if they sensed their fate.

One vendor displayed some pastry with a fruit filling that made Rachel's mouth water. She bought three and ate hers slowly, to savor the sweetness. Distracted by all the interesting things for sale, Rachel began to lag behind the others. She stopped when she came upon a boy selling a Yiddish newspaper called *Israel's Messenger*.

"How much for the newspaper?" Rachel asked the boy.

"Two fen," the boy replied.

Rachel squinted and saw Nucia and Menahem farther

down the road buying some tea. Making sure no one was watching, she reached into her pouch, pulled out two brass coins, and dropped them in the boy's outstretched palm. He handed her the newspaper, which she tucked under her arm. Then she ran to catch up with the others.

上海

"A laundry on Bubbling Well Road is hiring right now," Isaac announced at dinner. "This would be good for Shprintze and Rachel." He dipped his bun in black vinegar and looked at Shprintze.

Rachel gagged on a piece of dry bread in her mouth. Butter was rare in Shanghai and she didn't like the black vinegar, which seemed to be the custom here.

"Are you all right?" asked Isaac casting a concerned look at Rachel.

Rachel swallowed the lump, which went down her throat like a dry rag, and nodded.

"Isn't that wonderful news?" said Nucia. She cut her carp and put a piece in her mouth.

Rachel looked at Shprintze with a stricken expression.

"Are you sure?" asked Shprintze. "We have been to many places and nobody is hiring."

"A man I work with told me that his wife just got a job there," explained Jacob. "And they need three or four more women to help with the laundry they get from hotels."

"You must go early tomorrow morning," said Danka Muller, setting a bowl of lychee fruit in the center of the table. "Positions are scarce in this city."

A murmur of ascension rose from the other boarders at the table. Rachel's blood boiled as people she barely knew, strangers, intruded on her dismal future.

Shprintze shrugged apologetically at Rachel. "We will go early tomorrow morning."

Rachel stuffed the rest of her bun in her mouth and chewed vigorously until her jaw ached and she'd swallowed the last bite.

That night, unable to sleep, she pictured herself as a fifty-year-old laundress, still toiling away in Shanghai. Rachel crept out of bed and left the room, clutching her empty stomach to curb the rumbling sounds. She made her way down the creaky stairs and out the door, moving toward a nearby streetlamp. Her felt shoes squashed down the mud, which stuck to her feet like clay. Nighttime had become her favorite part of the day, the only time when the streets were quiet, when even the animals seemed to close their mouths. Twisting her head to make sure she was alone, Rachel pulled the newspaper out from the waist of her skirt and started to read.

The first article she read in *Israel's Messenger* discussed Zionism, a movement to create a Jewish national home in Palestine. Rachel remembered her father talking about Zionism at the dinner table. He didn't believe in Zionism because he thought that people of different faiths should live together peacefully. "Setting us apart from people of other faiths will only put up more borders between us," he'd said.

Rachel returned to the article and saw that the writer had some compelling arguments in favor of Zionism, explaining that a Jewish state would provide a safe homeland for displaced Jews like herself.

She continued to pour over the newspaper, scanning

articles about well-to-do Baghdadi Jews living in Shanghai: the Sasoons who owned hotels and sold Chinese silk, tea, and silver to companies outside of Shanghai; the Hardouns who were opening a new store; and the Kadoories, who had just started a new rickshaw company.

Such prosperous Jews! How did they get so much money and power? wondered Rachel.

By the time Rachel had finished reading the newspaper, she was exhausted. She trudged back to her room where she fell into a deep slumber.

上海

To Rachel's dismay, she and Shprintze got jobs at the laundry the next morning. In a stifling room, they learned how to wash bed linens and tablecloths in deep tubs of water, how to wring out fabric, and how to press linens with a hot, heavy iron.

"I wish I'd paid more attention when my mother tried to teach me to sew," said Rachel to Shprintze at the end of their first day. "For the first time, I envy Nucia sitting all day with a needle and thread." Pain tore through Rachel's neck as she turned her head toward Shprintze.

Shprintze opened and closed her red, swollen hands. "My skin is as dry as sand. I don't know if I'll be able to hold a glass of tea without dropping it."

"We must keep our eyes and ears open for other jobs," said Rachel, once they'd left the laundry. The pink evening sky pressed down on her shoulders, reminding her of the days and weeks that had gone by since they'd arrived, of her dream of making enough money to travel to America.

"But we looked for weeks before finding this one."
Shprintze shook her head. "We have no choice."

"There has to be something better," muttered Rachel.
"With the paltry wages we make here, it will take years to save
up for our passage to America."

9

September 28, 1903
Barracks No. 6
Putilov Factory
47, Stachek Avenue
Petersburg, Russia

My dearest Rachel,

Your letter made me smile for the first time in weeks.

I am so relieved to hear you and Menahem are safely out of Russia and pray your mother gets better soon. I worry that having Menahem is a burden for you and your family. I am afraid that I may have expected too much of you when I asked you to take him with you. Enclosed is a small amount of money to help with his food. I wish I could send more but my wages are poor.

I'm working in Petersburg, at the Putilov factory. (My mother sent your letter to me here, which took a week to arrive by train, and I expect it will be weeks before you receive this one, as it will have to go by train and steamer.) The factory spews black smoke day and night, and my throat is constantly sore. There are many factories near me, and the area seems like a different world from the center of Petersburg where there are many magnificent buildings.

I think fondly about our walks together. At night, before I fall asleep, I picture your face. I often think about the possibility of being with you and Menahem again.

Enclosed is a drawing of the Summer Garden for you and Menahem. I spend Sunday afternoons here amongst trees and fountains, and never tire of looking at the Neva River from this vantage point. Here, I can almost forget about the factory life for a little while.

Take care of yourself and write me as soon as you can,
Your Sergei

P.S. Thank you for sharing the Chinese symbols with me. They intrigued me with their shape and the way the lines formed a picture. One symbol looked like a house within a square. Do you know what it means?

"Thirty kopecks," said the shopkeeper, placing the paper, envelopes and inkbottle on the counter.

Sergei picked through the coins in his pouch until he had two ten-kopeck pieces and two fives. "Used to be twenty-five kopecks for writing paper and ink," he said. "I won't be able to send letters anymore if prices keep going up."

The shopkeeper scooped the coins off the counter and smirked out of the left side of his mouth. "Used to be that I could afford to eat, drink, and smoke. Now I have to choose one."

Sergei frowned and stuck his purchases into his satchel. He stepped through the door of the shop. The strong wind slapped his face as he strode to the factory.

"You just made it, country bumpkin," sneered a metalworking apprentice who wore high boots and a white shirt tied with a black sash.

The condescending way he spoke reminded Sergei of his father, who had constantly ridiculed him for wanting to be an architect instead of a policeman. Sergei loved to draw and had hoped to use his artistic talents to make a living. Now he scowled and picked up a handful of screws that had to be tested. He twirled the first screw and started to remove it when a loud cry sounded from the driller's station, directly behind Sergei. He craned his neck and gasped when he saw blood gushing from the man's right eye. Sergei dropped his screws and rushed over to help steady the injured worker who tottered back and forth.

Blood oozed down his face as Sergei moved behind the man and held his underarms.

"I'll get the doctor," someone called out, running toward the office.

"Hurry," yelled Sergei, watching the color drain from the injured worker's face.

"My eye, my eye!" he groaned, covering his bleeding eye with oil-stained hands.

"Hold on, the doctor's coming."

The man whimpered and hunched over. Sergei held him tighter.

The doctor arrived, followed closely by the man who'd fetched him.

"Not again," muttered the doctor, taking in the situation. He opened his satchel and removed a glass bottle and a white cloth. He poured a little fluid onto the cloth, and told the man to remove his hands from his face.

A crowd gathered, watching silently as the doctor treated the worker's injury. When the worker uncovered his eye, the onlookers moaned in unison; many turned away, their faces twisted in revulsion. Sergei was relieved he couldn't see the eye.

"All of you, back to work," announced the foreman, a brawny man with a tuft of auburn hair on his otherwise bald head.

The crowd dispersed and the factory soon began to clang steadily as the machines roared back to life.

The foreman addressed the doctor. "How long is this going to take?"

"I'm almost finished." The doctor attached a clean patch onto the worker's eye.

Sergei felt the patient flinch as the doctor worked.

"Is he going to see again?" asked the foreman.

The doctor looked squarely at the foreman. "Have any of the men injured by this machine regained their sight?"

"No, dammit."

The injured worker's legs gave way. Sergei braced his own legs and yanked the man up before he hit the ground.

"I've told them a hundred times to get this machine fixed!" The doctor stood back, surveyed his work, and shrugged. "Best I can do."

"Get him out of here," said the foreman, flicking his hand at the doctor. "And you—" he turned to Sergei. "Back to work. The doctor will take him from here."

The doctor stood beside the injured worker, and supported him at the waist. Sergei let go and fumbled with his screws while the foreman stood, hands on his hips, waiting for Sergei to resume his work.

上海

Two days later, Sergei felt as if someone were inspecting him as he twirled a screw around; his hand shook as he started to remove it. His elbow was suddenly shoved upwards and he dropped the screws. They scattered all over the floor, like rubles dropping onto a sidewalk.

"Sorry, my hand must have slipped," said the metalworking apprentice, looking around the factory with a grin of superiority. Apprenticeships were prized for their opportunity to advance as a tradesperson, which meant they could earn more money. They often looked down on ordinary workers who would never rise from their lowly status.

Sergei watched the screws spread across the floor and remembered when his father had come home drunk and had ripped a drawing he'd been working on for days into pieces. Rage ignited Sergei's veins; his skin grew warm and red.

"I think you're turning green," said the apprentice with a gloating smile. "Hey, Lev, don't you think Sergei looks green?"

Lev grunted and kept working, ignoring Sergei and the apprentice.

"You sure you're up to this job?" The apprentice moved in closer to Sergei. "You don't like getting your hands dirty, do you? I see the way you protect your hands, as if they're too good to be working here, as if they're better than mine."

The tops of Sergei's ears started to burn. He imagined his father calling him a coward again. Sergei clenched his jaw and bent down to pick up the screws.

"Stupid country bumpkin," said the apprentice. He kicked Sergei's rear end with the heel of his boot.

Every muscle in Sergei's body tightened until he grew as taut as a violin string. He released the screws from his fingers and, in one fluid motion, punched the apprentice in the chin, so hard that he fell against the drilling machine, cracking his head on the metal. The man groaned and cradled his head with his hands.

"Stupid country idiot," said the apprentice a couple of seconds later. He leaned forward with both fists and struck Sergei in the stomach. "Are you afraid to fight?"

Sergei held in a moan and cuffed the apprentice's ear. Once, then once again. A hot, black rush of anger pushed Sergei over the edge. He hit the apprentice's face over and over, until strong hands yanked him back.

"What the hell are you doing?" said the foreman, holding onto Sergei's shirt. "You're acting like a couple of school boys."

"He started it," announced the apprentice, still clutching his head. "Threw me for no reason."

"That's a lie," said Sergei. "Right, Lev?" Sergei stared at Lev, but Lev looked away, as if he didn't know Sergei.

"I ought to let you go," the foreman said to Sergei. "But we don't have enough men now, and there's more work than we can handle around here. So I'll take fifty kopecks from your pay instead. Understood?"

Sergei nodded. The man holding his shoulders let him go. Sergei spat on the ground as soon as the foreman turned his back.

"Remember, you're just a lowly country bumpkin, Khanzhenkov," growled the apprentice.

Sergei swallowed and picked up the screws. He watched the apprentice until he'd returned to his station.

"Sorry, about not backing you up," said Lev later, after the bell sounded, declaring the short meal break. He had caught up to Sergei, walking out of the factory toward the canteen in a nondescript building beside the factory.

Sergei kept his gaze straight ahead.

"It's best not to show we're friends, especially with me, you know."

"Doesn't matter," muttered Sergei as they stepped through the arched doorway that led to the canteen, a one-storey building with rows of tables and benches for seats.

"Be careful. Next time you won't be so lucky. You have to keep your mouth shut and avoid trouble."

"That's not so easy for me," said Sergei. "When the foreman told me he'd take fifty kopecks from my wages, I wanted to spit in his face."

Lev shrugged and sat down at a dark wood table.

Sergei sat across from him. The smell of onions and dense tobacco smoke clouded the air.

Lev took a couple of pieces of black bread from a serving

woman dressed in white with a white cap. "Getting mad at the foreman will get you nowhere but broke and out of work. You need to think bigger if you want to get back at management."

"If you're talking about striking again, forget it," said Sergei. "There were four strikes last week at factories in Moscow. The organizers were exiled to Siberia and the strikers lost their jobs." He took a bowl of watery soup from the serving woman, along with a glass of lukewarm tea.

"Maybe they sleep better at night in Siberia, knowing they did something." Lev shoved a piece of bread in his mouth and leaned in closer to Sergei. "We have to keep fighting, with larger numbers, more factories, to show the government we're not giving up, that we're getting stronger."

"Or there may be nobody left to work. We'll all be begging on the streets or doing hard labor in Siberia," said Sergei.

10

Rachel's head slumped forward. Her body slipped down the brick steps into the *mikveh* until her face became submerged. She gagged on the cool water, threw her head back and slowly got out of the mikveh, the ritual bath where Jewish women cleansed themselves before the Sabbath.

"I don't think I can stay awake for the Sabbath service," Rachel told Nucia when they went back to their room. "I almost drowned in the mikveh because I'm so tired."

Rachel threw herself face down on her cot. Her hair splayed out around her head. Menahem had already left for the synagogue with Isaac.

"We must go to *shul* on *shabes*. It's part of our Jewish tradition," said Nucia, sitting on the edge of the cot, brushing out Rachel's long, tangled hair.

"For weeks, while we traveled, we didn't observe shabes, say our prayers, or even eat kosher food. And nothing terrible happened to us," argued Rachel.

"What about Mother?" said Nucia. "She would want us to continue observing our traditions." She separated Rachel's hair into three equal sections to braid it.

Rachel jerked her head up, causing Nucia to lose control of the braid. "Do you think Mother became sick because she didn't attend shul, when we were on the train?" she said self-righteously.

"Hold still." Nucia pressed Rachel's head down, braiding her hair with her skillful hands. "I don't know. But I do know we neglected our faith. We could have spent our time reading our prayer book—"

"How can you even think this?" Rachel bolted up and shook her head to get rid of the half-finished braid. "We did what we had to do to survive. No religion worth following would punish people for not following the rules." Nucia rose from the cot and stepped back, gaping at Rachel as if she were seeing her for the first time.

Rachel waited for her sister to reply, but Nucia didn't open her mouth. As was often the case, they agreed to disagree. The two of them continued to get ready in silence, moving awkwardly around the small room like strangers.

Unable to resist a further act of defiance, Rachel left her hair loose, gathering looks of alarm as she took a seat on the bench beside Shprintze in the upper women's gallery of the Shearith Israel Synagogue. Isaac and Menahem sat below in the main prayer hall.

When the service began with a prayer, Rachel could barely sit up straight, let alone pay attention. The rabbi's chanting swirled around in her head like the unintelligible language she heard on the streets—for she, like most Jewish girls, had been taught Yiddish, not Hebrew, at her school in Kishinev and therefore had very little understanding of Hebrew. In Kishinev, only boys had attended *cheder*, the Hebrew school. She felt herself falling over. Nucia's elbow in her side jolted her back into an upright position, which she struggled to keep for the remainder of the service.

Back at the hostel, when Rachel lay down on her cot next to Menahem, she found slumber elusive. Her muscles throbbed and her mind raced with memories, dreams, and ideas. In due course, she drifted off to sleep, but when she woke up, felt just as tired.

The next morning, Rachel stirred when she heard a baby's cry from a nearby room. Morning light crept through the window, but Nucia and Menahem continued to sleep. When they awoke, they would return to the synagogue for morning prayers. Holding her breath so not to awake them, she made her way to the door, slipped on her felt boots, put on some clothes, and crept out of the room. Outside, the morning air cleansed her face, a brief respite from muggy, smelly afternoons. Rachel headed toward Nanking Street. The roads grew busier and louder the farther she walked. Rickshaws passed, sometimes so close that Rachel felt wind brushing on her skin.

When she turned onto Nanking Street, many people walked along the sidewalks, though the morning had just begun. She looked at the bold signs with Chinese characters hanging above the shops. Looking to the left and to the right, she continued down the street, taking in the vibrant silks hanging in front of several shops, magnificent in shades of red, green, and blue. She held out her hand to touch one that particularly interested her, but pulled it back quickly when a toothless Chinese woman appeared. The woman said something in Chinese that Rachel could not understand. It was not pleasant, judging from the woman's snarling face and angry hand gestures. Rachel backed away from the shop and walked down the street, her face red and her heart pounding. People seemed to stare at her because she looked different.

Panting and out of breath, Rachel slowed down a block from the angry silk vendor. She inhaled and exhaled three times, until her heart rate decreased. Looking back in the direction of the vendor, Rachel realized that she had probably overreacted. The woman's anger might not have been based on hate, but merely on preventing her from dirtying the expensive fabric.

She strolled down the street once more, but stopped when the delicious aroma of fried food drifted into her nose. On her right, a vendor sold greasy pastries and buns.

"How much?" she asked the vendor, a brittle-looking man with a sharp nose. She pointed at the buns.

He shrugged and spoke rapidly in his language.

Rachel sifted through the coins in her pouch and held one up.

He shook his head.

She held out two coins and he handed a bun to her.

Rachel continued down the bustling street, taking small bites of her bun, which tasted a bit like challah, except this had been fried in oil. When she finished, Rachel licked her lips and decided she liked it better than challah.

The street ended at a racecourse. The oval course stood empty and silent, in strong contrast to Nanking Street, and smelled strongly of manure. Rachel leaned against a gate for a few minutes, to watch for horses, but the course remained quiet.

She headed left and, within minutes, found herself in a different district of the city, the French Concession. With its tree-lined, broad street, Avenue Petain reminded her a little of Upper Kishinev, where the wealthy people had lived. Here, the buildings were all three storeys tall, and most had arched windows and doors as well as intricate moldings that Rachel admired.

Does Paris look like this? she wondered. *I wish I could draw a picture and send it to Sergei. He would be fascinated by this architecture.*

Rachel slowed her pace to stretch out her time in this almost-deserted area; only a couple of well-dressed men walked ahead of her. The leaves were starting to turn rich shades of ocher, ginger, and plum.

When Avenue Petain ended, Rachel turned left. She'd walked in a square from the hostel where she'd started to avoid getting lost, and found herself on the Bund, the business section of Shanghai. On the Rue du Consulat overlooking the Huangpu River, taller office buildings could be seen. Gazing at the windows above her, she wondered what people did inside, if they were distracted by the view of the river that changed as suddenly as the weather.

Today, the current looked strong, pushing *sampans*, the flat-bottomed wooden boats, roughly through the water, and boats tied to wharves rocked vigorously from side to side. Rachel walked through the small grassy space between the river and the road, to the riverbank. She knelt down, gathered a handful of stones and tossed them into the water, one by one, just as she'd done at the River Byk in Kishinev.

The sky had brightened, but Rachel couldn't return to the hostel unless she wanted to be dragged to the synagogue. She stood up, stretched her arms to the sky, and glanced over her left shoulder. The brick walls of the old city arose in the distance. She flicked a strand of hair behind her ear, smiled mischievously, and began walking.

Guards with shaved heads and long rifles slung over their left shoulders stood erect at the eastern gate of the old city. Except for the rifles, they looked less than menacing wearing tunics adorned with Chinese symbols and trousers that were wider at the feet than the waist. The twenty-foot wall towered over them, and the dark archway looked more foreboding than the men guarding it.

Chinese people, young and old, walked in and out of the gate, their gaze resting on Rachel for a moment, and then flitting away as if they too were being watched. Dressed in white and black, their garments loose and graceful, the men, women, and children seemed almost as if they were part of a procession.

Standing there, with the solid wall in front of her, Rachel recalled Aleksandrov Street in Kishinev which had divided Gentiles and Jews. Only this high wall presented an actual barrier, with its sturdy gate that blocked every foreigner out. Rachel pried her eyes from the gate and resumed walking.

上海

Looking up, Rachel noticed she'd come to the corner of Nanking Road and North Sichuan Road, which led to the harbor and the medical building that held quarantined people. Without hesitation, Rachel turned left.

"Please, let me see her for just five minutes," Rachel pleaded. She stood at the gate outside the entrance to the white medical building where her mother still lay in quarantine, months after their arrival.

The Chinese man in the long coat and brimmed straw hat shook his head and turned away from Rachel. She gripped the bars of the gate until her hands turned white. She pressed her face against the gate, determined to stay there until they let her in, even if it meant waiting all night. The man resumed his position beside the doorway leading into the medical building.

Rachel focused her gaze on him, begging him silently to take pity on her, and let her in. He looked in the opposite direction, as if she weren't even there. Rachel slunk down to her knees, her fingers still wrapped around the bars. The sky darkened and the air cooled. Still, she did not let go.

"Can I help you?" said a man's voice in Yiddish.

Rachel thought the voice was in her head, in a dream.

"Excuse me," the voice said, louder this time. "I understand you would like information about your mother?"

Rachel looked up to find a Jewish man, a doctor with a stethoscope around his neck, peering at her with concern from the other side of the gate. He had long earlobes and a pock-marked face.

"Are you all right?" he asked her.

"Yes." She stood. "I need to see my mother. She's been in there for two months and nobody will tell me anything!"

"Ita Paskar?"

"Yes."

He cleared his throat. "I'm afraid she's not improving."

A lump lodged in Rachel's throat.

"Her cough is very bad and she's quite weak." The doctor paused. "It's most definitely consumption; she won't get better."

"That's what they told me on the ship," said Rachel in a papery-thin voice. She dropped to the ground and wrapped her arms around her knees.

"I am sorry," said the doctor gently. He cleared his throat again.

"Can I see her?"

He considered this for a second. "I'm afraid this would be impossible. She's contagious, it's a miracle you didn't get the disease."

Tears flooded Rachel's eyes. "Will she be sent back to Russia?"

"I promise you she is resting comfortably and won't be sent back to Russia. She's too weak to travel."

Rachel rocked back and forth, her arms still wrapped around her knees.

The doctor continued speaking in a calm, reassuring tone, but his words meant nothing to her. Rachel wanted to squeeze through the gate, find her mother, and climb into bed beside her. "I don't care about being infected. I don't care about getting sick."

The doctor crouched down to her level. "You mustn't talk like that. Your mother wouldn't want you to give up, would she?"

Rachel looked up at him and stopped rocking. "My father is already gone. I don't want to live in a world without either of my parents."

"You are very persistent. I know you will survive, and I know that your parents would want you to stay strong."

Rachel exhaled wearily.

"Did you come here with people, family?" he asked her.

"My sister and my stepbrother."

"Then go to them, I'm sure they're worried about you."

Rachel slowly got to her feet. "I'm going to return, you know."

"I know you will." He gave her a tight-lipped smile and turned back toward the building.

11

On an overcast morning, before work, Rachel ventured into the International Settlement and its assortment of different races and backgrounds. Here she found a familiar Jewish presence—Abram's Dried Goods, a half-built synagogue, a Jewish market, and a small office tucked between a shoe store and a dress shop. A sign on the door said, "Israel's Messenger, Neb Ezra, Publisher." Rachel tentatively opened the door.

Inside, a man with a sallow complexion and a long, black beard sat behind tall stacks of books and papers on his desk.

"Yes, what is it?" he growled in Yiddish without looking to see who had entered.

Rachel breathed in the sharp, tinny ink smell and grew dizzy. She leaned against the door until the uncomfortable sensation passed. "Are you Mr. Ezra?" she asked him in Yiddish.

"That's right." Mr. Ezra had stopped writing and looked at Rachel with a penetrating gaze.

"I'm looking for a job," she said meekly.

"What's that? Speak up," he barked. "I didn't hear a word you said."

Rachel took a deep breath and stepped forward. "I said I'm looking for a job," she said again, louder.

He shook his head. "Already have a cleaning lady."

"I don't want to be a cleaning lady. I want to write."

"A writer? You say you want to be a writer?" He pressed his hands down on the edge of his desk and leaned forward, as if he were getting ready to pounce.

Rachel nodded and lifted her shoulders, standing as tall as possible.

"You're a child. You should be in school."

"I'll be fifteen in November." Rachel stuck out her chin.

Mr. Ezra leaned back but kept his hands perched on his desk. "I don't have time for this." He nodded his head toward the pile of papers in front of him.

"I really need work…my mother's ill and…"

"There're plenty of shops taking on seamstresses."

"I'm useless with a needle and thread." She took a deep breath. "I've read *Israel's Messenger* and could write stories about the Russian Jews in Shanghai. I don't think people just want to read about the rich Jews from Baghdad."

He scratched his head vigorously. "Does your father know you're here? Criticizing a hard-working, local business?"

"My father is dead." Rachel's voice broke as the words escaped her mouth.

"Oh."

"I have no money, no skills except writing. My father hoped I'd be able to go to university one day, so I attended a

Jewish girls' school in Kishinev where I learned how to write Yiddish really well. And I work very hard."

He propped his elbows on his desk, brought his hands together, and rested his chin in his hands. "I wish I could help you, but I can't take a chance on an inexperienced girl. And, to be perfectly honest, I don't think my readers would be interested in reading articles written by women."

Rachel bit her lower lip and nodded.

"I'm sure you'll find something more suitable here. Shanghai is growing like carp in the spring."

Rachel sniffed back her tears and stepped closer to Mr. Ezra. "If I did write something, would you read it?"

"Just my luck," groaned Mr. Ezra, holding his palms up to the ceiling. "She's stubborn as a wild boar." He gave Rachel a long, hard stare. "I can't promise anything. I'm a busy man, but if I have the time, I'll look at it."

Rachel's heart pounded. "You won't be disappointed."

上海

The hot water steamed Rachel's face as she leaned over the tub and kneaded the linen with both hands. Her shoulders throbbed and the raw, cracked skin on her knuckles stung when soap grazed her pores. Worst of all…the boredom, the mind-numbing repetition. Rachel stared at the fabric, twisted and mangled in the soapy water, and tried to think of something to write about for Mr. Ezra. But her mind remained as blank as a fresh sheet of paper. She pushed the bed sheets farther down and watched the water swirl around them. She needed to come up with a good story idea, something that would interest hundreds of readers.

Rachel's memory strayed back to Kishinev and the fraudulent anti-Jew headlines in the *Bessarabetz* that had fired up the Russians and ignited the pogrom: "Jews belonged to a secret society and could not be trusted." "Jews had found a new way to make wine without grapes which threatened to destroy the entire wine industry." "As Easter approaches, we need to come together, fellow Christians, to purge our town of Jews."

Rachel cringed as she recalled these scathing words that had no facts behind them, only hatred. These deceitful stories were the reason she wanted to be a journalist, to tell the truth about the Kishinev pogrom, to show people that Jews were fundamentally the same as other people, despite different beliefs and traditions.

She pulled a dripping bed sheet from the tub of cloudy water and began wringing it out with her hands, twisting it into a thick coil. *I cannot give up on my dream of becoming a writer,* she thought as her fingers maneuvered the fabric. *I need to work hard here in Shanghai and save my money so that I can travel to America where I can continue my education and broaden my knowledge. Then I will become a respectable journalist. This is my mission.*

She began to daydream: an image of the *Israel's Messenger* emerged in Rachel's mind. She saw a front-page story, with a big photo and headline. Her name appeared under the headline: By Rachel Paskar. She scrunched her face to see the words but they were illegible.

"What are you doing?"

The laundry manager's thundering voice awakened Rachel from her fantasy. She dropped the sheet back into the tub.

"You've been holding one sheet for five minutes," the manager continued. "If this work is too hard, you can leave."

He stood so close to her she could smell the herring on his breath.

"No," said Rachel. She scooped up the sheet and wrung it out energetically. "I will stay late to wash my share and more."

The manager grunted and watched her wring out the fabric, hang it to dry, and reach for the next sheet. He tapped his foot on the ground as she worked, which made her tense and nervous. *I can't take this much longer*, she fretted. Under the manager's shrewd eyes, Rachel finished wringing out the linen in her tub. But as she thrust her hands into the water, she thought longingly of the ocean that would one day carry her to America.

上海

"How long have you been here?" Rachel asked Danka Muller. Rachel and Danka stood in the back room on the first floor, where Danka boiled water for tea. The small room contained a porcelain basin, a square table, and a stove. Outside, clothes hung perfectly still from a string for there was not even a hint of wind.

"You mean in Shanghai?" said Danka, her voice raspy from the countless cigarettes she smoked every day.

"Yes."

"Two years, I think." She looked up and pinched her lips together for a second. There were fine black hairs above her upper lip. "That's right. Two years."

Rachel wrote this down in her journal. "And why did you come here?"

"Same as everyone else, to get out of Russia."

"Why did you want to get out of Russia?"

"Same as you, I think. Because hoping and waiting for better days makes fools of all of us."

Rachel bit her bottom lip to keep from screaming. These answers weren't a story. Danka said nothing new, nothing interesting that readers would want to hear about. "Tell me the hardest part about coming here?" she prodded.

Danka poured boiling water into the samovar while holding a lit cigarette. She inhaled, then exhaled circles of smoke. "Leaving my home. It wasn't much, one room for Max and me. But it was ours." Her voice dropped as she spoke, as if she were imagining herself back in her house. "I did bring the samovar all the way across Russia, though it caused bitter words between us. He called me crazy for lugging such a heavy thing across the country. But it had been my mother's." Danka stopped and gazed lovingly at the metal samovar.

Rachel followed her gaze and stared at the metal samovar, which looked like an ordinary teapot to her. Nothing special. She thought about her father's violin, how ordinary it seemed, yet she'd kept a fragment. She had an idea: *This is my story. I'll write about the belongings people brought with them, what they couldn't live without, how we're all holding onto pieces of our past.*

Rachel scribbled a few more notes about the samovar and went off to find another hostel resident.

12

Since losing my home in Kishinev, I've been carrying around a piece of my father's violin and his tallis. Though these objects cannot help provide for me and my family in Shanghai, they are irreplaceable reminders of my father, killed during the riots. When I touch the fragment of his violin, I can almost hear him playing a gentle melody on a cold winter evening. It's as if a part of him is still here with me.

In speaking to other people who have come to Shanghai from Russia, I discovered that they also took items with them with which they could not be parted. Danka Muller, who runs a hostel with her husband Max Muller, brought her cherished samovar.

"I did bring the samovar all the way across Russia, though it caused bitter words between me and Max," she told me. "He called me crazy for lugging such a heavy thing across the country, but it had been my mother's."

Now, while her samovar bubbles all day long, Danka is

reminded of her mother and her former life in Russia, before the troubles began.

Yiehl Mendelssohn, who turned sixty last month, keeps his tin whistle in his waist pouch at all times.

"I gave this whistle to my son when he turned thirteen, but he and my wife died soon after," said Yiehl Mendelssohn. "My son never learned to play it, a pity because he was very musical. He and his mother would often sing together in the evenings, bringing great joy to me. When I was forced to leave my home, I took only this whistle because it was so easy to carry. But it became more than a memory of my son. Without food or money, I began to play the whistle at train stations and in front of markets. People would throw me a few kopecks or a piece of bread or a handful of cherries. My tin whistle helped me travel across Russia to safety here in Shanghai."

Anna Levi traveled all the way from Siberia with three photos of her parents and a set of her mother's Sabbath candles. In Anna's favorite photo, her mother is sitting with her five sisters in front of a cherry tree.

"This photo was taken just before my mother married my father," Anna said to me. "It was the last photo of her and her sisters together. Someday, I hope to show this photo to my children so that they can see where they came from and what their grandmother looked like as a young woman."

These are just a few of the many stories that I've heard and although the objects people carried here have little monetary value, they are priceless because of the precious memories they hold.

Shanghai is a stepping stone, not a final destination for most of us. Our future is unknown and as unpredictable as the pogroms that forced many of us from our homes. One day, we will move on to different and better lives. But we must not forget where our roots lie, and we must tell our children and grandchildren about our past. This is when these photos, candles, and samovars will become irreplaceable treasures.

Mr. Ezra stroked his whiskers thoughtfully and glanced down at Rachel's story. Rachel, sitting in a chair facing Mr. Ezra's desk, began to breathe so quickly she started to feel faint.

"For whom did you write this?" he asked her finally, after what seemed to Rachel an eternity.

"People…people who've come here from…other places," said Rachel, tripping over her words.

"My readers are intelligent, well-read Jews from Baghdad and eastern Europe. Why do you think they would be interested in this story?"

"Because—"

"You think readers want to re-live the past?"

"I don't know."

"Too sentimental," said Mr. Ezra. "Reads more like a bedtime story than news."

"I thought it would be nice for people to see that they're not alone, that we've all gone through the same experiences," said Rachel, the words gushing out of her mouth.

Mr. Ezra leaned back and folded his hands behind his head. "Do you have any idea what it costs to produce an issue of *Israel's Messenger*?"

Rachel shook her head and bit her bottom lip.

"Do you think I have extra space just waiting for nice articles that don't actually provide important information?"

Rachel shook her head again.

Mr. Ezra dropped his hands and swung forward, leaning

on his desk. "I don't mean to be so hard on you, but this is a tough business, with no room for nostalgia."

"I understand."

"My readers want information that can help them be successful here in Shanghai, stories about controversial issues, like how new taxes or laws will affect the Jewish community."

Rachel swallowed and nodded. She stood and turned toward the door.

"It's well-written," Mr. Ezra called out as she neared the door. "I'll give you that. You know how to write."

Rachel opened the door and with her head held high, moved briskly down the street, her vision blurred by tears and by the heavy rain that had begun while she was speaking to Mr. Ezra. "How could I be so stupid?" she sobbed aloud as she walked, oblivious to rain and the curious stares from passersby. "I may never get another chance. I am such an idiot." A powerful gust of wind smacked Rachel from behind, almost knocking her off her feet. Awnings above shops, blown out of their supports, flapped against buildings. One, completely detached from its frame, whooshed past Rachel's head. The air sounded menacing as the wind gained speed and muscle.

With her skirt pressed against her thighs, Rachel ran along the sidewalk, already starting to flood. Shops barricaded their doors and windows and the rain continued to pelt Rachel's head. Her feet sloshed in her felt shoes as she hurried home. Hats, birds, leaves, and newspapers roared by, propelled by the wind.

By the time Rachel reached the hostel, her clothes were drenched through to her skin. She dashed up the stairs, yanked the door open, and slammed it behind her.

"A typhoon," she said breathlessly to Shprintze and Nucia, who were laying wet garments near the stove to dry.

"You're soaked," said Nucia. "Take off your wet things before you catch a chill."

Rachel peeled off her shoes and coat.

"Where have you been?" asked Shprintze. "Menahem has been asking for you."

Mr. Ezra's words echoed in Rachel's head: *Reads more like a bedtime story than news…but it's well-written.*

"I was learning about what it takes to be a writer," said Rachel. Ignoring the puzzled looks on Nucia and Shprintze's faces, she raced up the stairs, her wet skirt leaving puddles on every step.

PART THREE
Winter/
Spring 1904

*Among the Jews of Southern Russia, the feeling is that
whatever race is spared by the Government in the orders
to proceed to the front it will not be the Jewish.*

—The New York Times, *February 25, 1904*

13

Winter and the New Year arrived with snow and colder air, though it was not nearly as frigid or snowy as Russia in January. In fact, shop owners in Shanghai easily swept the snow away from their doors, whereas in Kishinev an ordinary snowfall would leave three feet or more on the ground.

It has been five months since she started working at the laundry, thought Rachel, as she kneaded white shirts through the soapy water in the basin. Her hands swelled at her fingertips and knuckles. On the floor beside her, stood a barrel filled with dirty clothes. Although ten female laundresses worked in the well-lit room, it was quiet, except for the sounds of water sloshing through fabric. The manager, a long-necked man with a shiny face, moved around the room stealthily, like a cat preparing to pounce.

"I'm worn out already and we have many more hours to go," said Anna, another Jewish refugee from Russia who lived

in the same hostel as Rachel. She was in Shanghai by herself, because her husband, like many other Jewish men, had
been drafted into the Russian army before they could leave the
country. Her arms were full of stiff, frozen bedding that she'd
removed from the line outside, and loose wisps of hair curled
from the humidity.

Shprintze, standing in front of a table with garments piled
higher than her head, folded each item, one at a time.

Rachel watched the dirt swirl around the soapy water and
sighed. "I try to think about something else when I'm here. Like
sitting around our bubbling samovar, my whole family, back in
Kishinev…" She shivered and pulled her shawl tighter around
her shoulders.

Anna began to stack the solid, frozen sheets on a large,
rectangular table. "I received a letter from my husband yesterday.
He's been stationed at Port Arthur, in Manchuria, and he says
the conditions are dreadful. There is not enough food or sup-
plies, yet more men and boys arrive every day."

"I'm so relieved we were able to get Menahem out of
Russia," said Rachel. "As an orphan, he might have been drafted
when he turned twelve, and forced to attend military school
until he reached eighteen. He'd have to serve twenty-five years."

"I know," said Shprintze. "I'm worried about my brother.
So far, the Russian military seems to have forgotten he exists."

"They might remember him soon," said Anna. "My husband says there is a strong chance of war against the Japanese
because both Russia and Japan want control over Port Arthur."

"Why?" asked Rachel.

"Russia needs a warm water seaport for trade. Unlike the
port of Vladivostok, where the water freezes over in the cold

months, Port Arthur can be used for shipping goods to other countries throughout the year because of its warmer climate. And Japan wants the port for themselves," explained Anna.

Shprintze listened to the discussion, then suddenly brought her hand over her mouth as if she was going to be sick.

"Are you all right?" Rachel dropped the shirt back into the water and rushed over to her friend. She put her hand on Shprintze's back and rubbed her gently.

Shprintze hung her head and tears fell from her eyelashes. "I'm going to have a baby."

"What? Are you sure?" said Anna.

Shprintze nodded. "I—we can't afford the doctor, but I'm certain. In April, I think."

"Oh." Rachel felt Shprintze's bony spine beneath her hand and wondered if her friend would be strong enough to carry a child. "Does Isaac know?"

Shprintze shook her head and wiped tears from her face, which suddenly looked older and worn out. "Every morning I wake up and hope that I've been mistaken, or that..." She turned her head away.

Even though Shprintze didn't finish her sentence, Rachel knew what she'd been thinking. Back in Kishinev, girls who had married very young and were pregnant often lost their babies or gave birth to dead ones.

"You have to tell Isaac," said Rachel.

Anna nodded her head in agreement.

"I know." Shprintze gazed down at her belly and rubbed it in a circle. "Before long it will be obvious."

The sound of a throat clearing startled Rachel. She turned and saw the manager glaring at her.

"Is there a reason why you've stopped working?" he asked her with a sneer. "Have you finished washing all the dirty clothes? Is there nothing for you to do?"

"No, sir," replied Rachel, looking him in the eye. "But my friend is not feeling well. I will finish her work and mine if she's allowed to go home and rest."

The manager glanced at Shprintze and then returned his gaze to Rachel. "If she goes home, she cannot return. I have many girls and women who would love to have her job." He clasped his hands behind his back and moved off.

"I'm feeling much better now," said Shprintze. She resumed folding but every few minutes a sob escaped her lips.

Rachel went back to her cold and slimy basin of water. Shprintze would be all right to work today and tomorrow, she thought. But in a couple of months, when the baby inside her had grown, her friend wouldn't be able to manage the heavy barrels and the long hours.

At the end of the day, Rachel trudged home under gray skies; she hadn't seen the sun in weeks, which increased her gloomy outlook. She watched Shprintze from the corner of her eye to see how pregnancy had changed her. Though her belly had not yet swelled, Shprintze carried herself differently, with rounded shoulders as if she were protecting the new life growing within her. And while Shprintze's face looked tense, her skin glowed.

"I'm sure Isaac will take the news well," said Rachel, when they arrived at the boarding house. "A baby is a good thing, a new beginning," said Rachel.

"Yes, but I'm afraid to tell him," said Shprintze in a meek voice.

"Things will work out in the end," said Anna. "This is what I tell myself every day when I worry about my husband."

They went to their rooms to wash for supper. The evening meal had become the best part of the day for Rachel, a time when everyone in the hostel gathered and talked about everything except the circumstances that led them to Shanghai. *In a way, we've become like a large family*, thought Rachel as she watched the residents take their places on the benches around the supper table. Jacob, a skinny young man with big ears, sat beside Nucia, who blushed when he spoke to her. Jacob came from a *shtetl* in Kiev in the Jewish Pale of Settlement, like Kishinev within the Russian Empire. He and Nucia had been spending many evenings together.

Tonight, Nucia had coiled her braid into an elegant bun so that her high cheekbones were more prominent. She looked beautiful and more relaxed than usual. As she talked to Jacob, her whole face lit up. All the tension that usually clouded Nucia's face disappeared when she spent time with Jacob. Rachel thought to herself, *if we were still in Kishinev, Nucia might be engaged or married to a stranger, a man or boy of the same social and financial status—someone chosen by a professional matchmaker. Nucia and the groom would have little say in the matter. This is better, Nucia becoming friends with Jacob because she likes him.*

Yehiel Mendelssohn, a senior at the hostel, sat at the end of the table. His face looked wrinkled and blotted with age spots and his hand shook constantly. Anna sat next to Yosef Trumpeldor, a young dentist from Siberia with curly hair and whiskers. Across the table sat two middle-aged sisters who hardly ever spoke a word.

When Danka Muller entered the room and placed large platters of bread, fish, beets, and cabbage in the middle of the table, Rachel realized that Shprintze and Isaac had not appeared. She caught Anna's eye and mouthed, "Shprintze." Anna shrugged her shoulders. Danka Muller sat down beside her husband, Max, and Yehiel Mendelssohn chanted the blessing before the meal. Rachel stared at the two empty seats and worried that Isaac might be upset about Shprintze's pregnancy.

Meanwhile a lively discussion began around the dinner table. "I read in the paper today that some five hundred Jewish soldiers have deserted the Russian army," said Yehiel Mendelssohn. He ate a forkful of cabbage. A piece dribbled from the side of his mouth as he chewed.

"That's terrible!" said Yosef Trumpeldor, dropping his knife. "Leaving the army makes all of us Jews look like cowards."

"How can you say that?" asked Anna. "Don't you know how badly Jewish soldiers are treated by the Russians? My husband says if a Jew is late for duty, he's treated as a deserter, and that almost all the Jews in his regiment are put in dangerous combat positions. If there's a war, they'll serve at the front and face the most peril."

"Jews should be proud to defend their country," argued Yosef. "And soldiers do benefit from their service. They're no longer exiled to the Pale of Settlement, but can live in the cities where they served once their term is over."

"That's not entirely true," interjected Yehiel Mendelssohn. "Soldiers are still forbidden to live in Russian capital cities like Petersburg or Moscow."

Footsteps on the stairs ended the discussion.

"I'm sorry we're late," said Isaac as he entered the room.

Right behind him stood Shprintze, her face pale and drawn.

Isaac took his place beside Menahem and Shprintze sat down beside her husband.

Rachel tried to catch Shprintze's eye during the meal, but Shprintze kept her head lowered and said nothing while she ate. Later, when everyone else had returned to their rooms, Shprintze, Anna, and Rachel had a moment to themselves in front of the stove.

"Are you all right?" Rachel asked Shprintze.

Shprintze dangled her stocking feet in front of the flickering fire. "Isaac took the news better than I expected, but he's anxious about providing for another person."

"It won't be easy," said Anna.

"All the money we've saved to go to America will have to be spent on the doctor now, and on food and clothing for the baby," said Shprintze. She sniffed and rubbed her nose. "You'll have to write to me when you go to America, Rachel, and tell me what it's like."

Rachel clasped Shprintze's hands and gave her an earnest look. "You mustn't give up hope. One day you will come to America with Isaac and your child."

Shprintze leaned her head against Rachel's shoulder and stared at the glowing flames.

上海

"Hurry, Menahem," called Rachel when she reached Tong Shan Road. She waited as Menahem walked behind her, dragging his feet as if they were treading through mud. "We're both going to be late." Rachel shivered and pulled her shawl tighter around her shoulders. On the corner, a homeless man lay in a heap on the frost-covered ground.

Rachel stopped and waited for Menahem. He quickened his pace slightly. A couple of boys, taller than Menahem, passed him, knocking his shoulder as they strode by. Rachel opened her mouth to admonish the boys, but Menahem acted as if he hadn't noticed them.

On the frozen river, young people glided across the ice on horse-drawn sleighs. The passengers sat in chairs in front of the drivers, bundled in furs to keep warm. Exuberant voices echoed across the glistening surface, reminding Rachel of the carefree life she once had, of days filled with school and ice skating.

"Why do you insist on walking so slowly?" asked Rachel, when Menahem reached her, his face shiny and red. "It should only take us ten minutes but we've been walking for almost twenty."

He shrugged. They continued walking until they came to his school on Xinzha Road. The Shanghai Jewish School looked more like a church with its arched windows and ornate façade. Children gathered in clumps in front of the building.

"Do you think Sergei will ever come to Shanghai?" asked Menahem suddenly.

Rachel's hand went into her pocket where she felt for Sergei's most recent letter folded tightly into the palm of her hand, which she couldn't bear to put in her pouch with the others. "I think he wants to be here, but his family needs him in Russia. You know that."

Menahem slammed his foot down on a patch of ice. Lines appeared, cracks that stretched like shadows, long and thin.

Rachel crouched down bringing her face to the same level as his. "Things aren't easy for Sergei right now."

"What do you mean?"

"He's working at a factory but he wants to go to school and he's all alone in Petersburg with no family. He has to act like a man, even though he's so young. And every day he has to get up and do things he doesn't want to do."

"Is working at a factory as bad as working in a laundry?"

Rachel's face flushed with remorse. "You shouldn't have to listen to me moan about my job. I promise I won't complain anymore if you don't grumble about school and Sergei not being here."

"I'm sorry."

Rachel brushed a tear from his cheek. "For what?"

He wiped his face with the back of his hand. "I'm the man of our family now. I shouldn't complain. I'm not a baby."

Rachel struggled to keep her twitching mouth still. "You *are* the man of our family, which is why you need to learn everything you can."

"All right." He looked over his shoulder at the school, and turned back to Rachel. "Mother Ita's not going to get better, is she?"

"It doesn't look like it," said Rachel softly. "They haven't let me in to see her, but she doesn't seem to be improving."

"What if you get sick, or Nucia?"

"I can't promise that won't happen, but I can tell you that we never want to leave you." She opened her arms and gave Menahem a long hug.

When he pulled away, his bottom lip quivered.

"I'll see you tonight," she told him.

Menahem traipsed slowly through the gate, into the yard.

Rachel watched Menahem meet his friend and march into school with the other children. He'd become comfortable in Shanghai. It would be hard to pull him away from a place for the second time in his short life, if they ever did save enough money to go to America.

She pulled her shawl tighter around her neck, continued down Shaanxi Road and turned right onto Nanking Road. Jewish shops lined both sides of the street, including a three-storey market and a theater. Shopkeepers swept the snow from their doorways. A red-faced boy sold copies of *Israel's Messenger* at the corner.

Rachel took out two fen to pay for the newspaper. Though she felt bad spending money on something as frivolous as a newspaper, she appeased her guilt by telling herself that she needed to read the newspaper if she wanted to make a living as a writer.

She scanned the headlines on the first page. When she turned to the second page, she stopped suddenly—there was her story about people's journeys to Shanghai but her name was missing. There was no name at all. Numb, like a disoriented sheep, she read every word, noting that her original story had been cut in places, probably to fit in the space available. *Why didn't he put my name next to my words?* Rachel folded the paper, tucked it under her arm, and marched down the street, already thinking about what she would say to Mr. Ezra.

At the very end of the road stood a small, windowless building with a door on the side: The Shanghai Jewish Laundry. She sighed, opened it, and stepped into the oppressive, humid room where she would scrub clothes for the next twelve hours. After work, she would visit Mr. Ezra.

上海

"I thought you said nostalgia had no place in your newspaper," said Rachel to Mr. Ezra.

Mr. Ezra stood with a younger man in front of an array of photos. Both men looked up as Rachel spoke. Mr. Ezra said something quietly to the man and sauntered toward Rachel.

"We had extra space, so I inserted your article. You should be thanking me," he said.

"But my name isn't on it! Nobody will know I wrote this story."

Mr. Ezra held out his palms. "What can I say? People will not read a story written by a girl. The newspaper world is a man's world."

"I can write as well as a man," argued Rachel. "You wouldn't have printed my story if you didn't like it!"

"True, but even I was surprised by your talent."

Rachel's heart leaped at Mr. Ezra's words. *Your talent!* But instead she said, "You should've put my name on it."

"You must trust me," Mr. Ezra continued. "If my readers discovered a story written by a young woman, they would question its value or even worse, ignore it entirely."

Rachel mulled over Mr. Ezra's explanation, and decided that seeing her words in print was the best thing that had happened to her in months. "Will you write me a note saying that I wrote this story?"

Mr. Ezra's lips twitched upward. "I'll type it myself on

Israel's Messenger stationery." He took a crisp sheet of paper from a pile on his desk, inserted it into his typewriter, pulled his sleeves up, and began typing.

"Don't forget to include the date it was published and the issue number," said Rachel, gaping at the machine, the first she'd ever seen close up. The silver keys flung up and struck the paper while a black mechanism, shaped like a log, moved from side to side.

Mr. Ezra stopped typing and met her gaze. "I won't forget." He resumed typing for another minute, extracted the paper, and reviewed what he'd typed. Then he handed the note to Rachel.

She examined the letter and handed it back to him. "Can you sign it please?"

Mr. Ezra scrawled his name and pushed the paper toward Rachel. "Anything else?"

"I want to write again for the paper."

Mr. Ezra chuckled and stroked his beard. "I can't promise it will be published, but I would like to see more of your work."

She turned to leave.

"Wait!" said Mr. Ezra. He moved over to his desk, opened the top drawer, and counted out some coins. "Don't forget your payment," he said as he walked back to Rachel. He dropped five jiao into Rachel's hand.

Rachel stared in disbelief at the shiny coins.

"Spend it wisely," said Mr. Ezra.

Rachel shook her head. "I'm saving it for my passage to America."

"I'm afraid you'll need much more than that for your journey."

"I know. I'll be back with another story soon."

14

Sergei's mouth watered as he walked past vendors selling spiced tea, Christmas cakes, sweet Vyborg *cracknels*, biscuits, and fruit *pastils*, hard candies. It was the seventh of January, the Russian Christmas Eve, but he couldn't bear to go to church with Lev and the rest of his fellow workers. Instead, he came to the Gostinny Dvor, the vibrant marketplace on the Nevsky Prospekt, to be away from his regimented life, to try to feel a trace of this festive season.

Sergei looked up into the sky that glittered with stars. At home in Kishinev, *sochevnïk*, the Holy Supper, would have begun after the first star had been spotted, in remembrance of the Star of Bethlehem. Hay would be spread on the floor and tables to represent the manger, and his sister would probably be making clucking noises to ensure a bountiful supply of eggs in the coming year. A tall white candle would flicker in the middle of the table as his family went through the twelve courses in honor of the twelve apostles.

They'd eat, open presents, and then go to church until two or three in the morning. A lump grew in Sergei's throat as he recalled the traditions he'd enjoyed since he was a child. This would be his first Christmas away from home, his first one spent amongst strangers, and he wondered if he'd ever celebrate Christmas with his family again.

He hoped his sister liked the pink shawl he'd sent her, and that his mother would have time to sit and enjoy the light from the candles he'd bought for her. For his father, he sent nothing.

Sergei stopped in front of a display of Christmas trees on the Nevsky Prospekt, simple and natural without candles or decorations. He inhaled the pine scent and the warmth of the season washed over him. Seeing a street vendor selling *kuetya*, boiled wheat sweetened with honey and sprinkled with poppy seeds, he bought a bowl. He ate it as he strolled down the street, savoring every mouthful even though it didn't taste nearly as good as his mother's.

This year will be better, he told himself as he waited for the trolley. His feet sank into the deep, heavy snow. *I will work hard, save money, and find out about taking courses at the university. Things will start falling into place for me.*

上海

A week after Christmas, Sergei reached into the machine with his right hand and tried to pry the releasing screw loose from the coupling mechanism but it didn't budge.

"Dammit," he muttered. He scrunched down under the mechanism to get a better view. The machinery had begun to rust, turning an orange-brown in places.

He grabbed the screw again and twisted his hand left. A clang shattered the air, like the sound of knives falling onto the ground. Sergei tried to yank his hand away, but it wouldn't budge. He pulled it as hard as he could, but it had become wedged between two solid parts of the machinery. The mechanism roared to life abruptly. A scorching pain shot through Sergei's hand.

"Lev, I'm stuck!" he called out.

Lev spun around from his station and dashed over to Sergei.

"My hand," screamed Sergei. "It's cutting my hand!"

Blood dripped down Sergei's forearm.

"Turn the coupling machine off!" shouted Lev to the foreman. "Now!"

Lev peered up into the machine, wrapped his hand around Sergei's arm, but couldn't move it an inch.

"The coupling machine, switch it off," Lev yelled again. "Fetch the doctor."

The foreman, who'd finally heard Lev's cries for help, turned from his conversation with another worker, ran over to the machine, and flicked off the power switch. The machine whirred to a halt and Sergei's hand released.

"Oh, that's nasty," said Lev, when Sergei's gnarled, bloody hand appeared like a young bird mauled to death by a magpie.

Sergei's head spun. His hand throbbed and the sight of it made him feel faint. He started to fall over, but Lev held him upright.

"That's a mess, all right," said the foreman, shaking his head and staring at Sergei's hand.

"We have to stop the bleeding," said the doctor, who surfaced with his worn black bag. He set it down, pulled out a roll
of white gauze bandage, and began to wrap Sergei's hand.

Sergei could feel pressure from the bandage, but it seemed
as if he were watching someone else being treated. Blood leaked
through the gauze, a spot that grew bigger and bolder.

He let Lev and the doctor maneuver him to the medical
room, a small, windowless space off the corridor, just outside the
factory. He felt his body lowered onto a cot. All around him,
men groaned, their jarring bass voices forming an incongruous
harmony. The strong antiseptic odor made his nostrils prickle.
As the doctor unwound the bandage, the pressure on his hand
loosened. Sergei diverted his eyes from his bloody hand and
attempted to slow his breathing, but a sudden stinging sensation
made him cry out. The doctor, seated on a stool beside his cot,
had begun cleaning his hand with carbolic acid.

The doctor didn't even flinch when he heard Sergei moan.

Sergei caught a glimpse of his hand; his skin had been torn
right down the middle of his palm. His throat constricted. He
looked away and saw another man lying in the cot beside him,
his head bandaged so that only his face was visible. There were
a dozen injured men in the small room, with injuries of vary-
ing degrees. The air was thick with the metallic scent of blood.

A piercing pain made Sergei cry out again. He turned
toward the doctor and saw him stitching the jagged gash with
a needle and black thread. The doctor's tongue hung out of
one side of his mouth like a dog's as he sewed the flaps of skin
together.

"Hold still," the doctor ordered, "or you'll make it worse."

Sergei gritted his teeth and gazed at the ceiling until the

doctor had finished stitching the wound and had bandaged it up again.

"That should do," the doctor said, rising from his seat.

"How long until I can return to work?" croaked Sergei.

The doctor smoothed his whiskers and sighed. "A couple of weeks, maybe three. But even when the skin heals, your hand won't move as well as it did before."

"But I'll be able to work, won't I?" asked Sergei.

"Too soon to tell," the doctor replied. He moved down the row of cots and checked on another worker whose foot and shin were bandaged.

Sergei tried to bend his fingers, but even a little movement made it feel as if his hand had been ripped open all over again. He stared at his useless hand, his shoulders hunched in defeat.

上海

"You realize you won't be paid while you're out of work," said Lev.

Sergei had returned to the barracks the day after his hand had been mangled. The two of them sat across from each other on their cots.

"What do you mean? I was injured working *here*," said Sergei.

"Doesn't matter. If you don't work, you don't get paid."

"But the machine is old and broken!"

"The factory makes the rules and there's nothing you can do."

"Nothing?"

"Well, you could strike for changes to these crazy rules."

"You mean join the Revolutionary Party?"

Lev shrugged. "It's the only way to get their attention."

Sergei looked down at his hand, which still ached. "I don't know, the factory treats us horribly. But the Revolutionary Party seems so extreme."

"The factory owners have forced the party to become radical, and I'm pretty sure we'll have to take even harsher measures before things get better."

"I don't really have much choice, do I?" said Sergei, looking at his mauled hand. "If I can't do my job at the factory, I don't know how I'll survive."

Lev glanced over both shoulders and spoke in a lowered voice. "We're planning a strike soon. If you're nervous about being seen at a meeting, just come to the strike. We need people to fill the streets, to show the government that our movement is growing and gaining strength."

"I suppose it would be hard for officers to remember a face in a crowd," said Sergei, mulling over his words. He met Lev's gaze. "And maybe this will be the strike that matters, that changes things for the better."

15

February 4, 1904
Barracks Number 6
Putilov Factory
47, Stachek Avenue
Petersburg, Russia

Dear Rachel,

I desperately wish I could be in Shanghai with you and
Menahem instead of in this dreary factory. I injured my
hand in the factory and am not sure I'll be able to keep
my job as I can only work at half my normal speed. Yet I
dread having to return to Kishinev as a failure, unable
to provide for my sister and mother, unable to save money
for university in Petersburg.

Enclosed is a picture I drew as I remember you,

sitting amongst the blooming wildflowers in Kishinev.
I drew it before I injured my hand. Your face is serene,
the way I remember you. Looking at it reminds me of
who I used to be.

Now I need to forget about the past and think of a
new path for myself. I hope this path will lead to you and
Menahem, that we can all be together one day soon, in a
place without fear or hatred.

As ever, Sergei

P.S. Please send me more Chinese symbols.

"I'm still not sure about striking at a different factory," said
Sergei to Lev. "It seems like a big risk to strike for workers we
don't even know."

The two of them walked from their barracks to the
Ekaterinoslav factory, two miles away. The black sky was deceiv-
ing, for it was just nine o'clock in the morning. January days
were the shortest of the year; the sun would not rise until eleven
o'clock, and would set before six o'clock. Sergei pulled up the
collar of his coat to stave off the frigid January air. A gust of
wind blew through his thin coat, sending chills up and down
his spine. His bandaged hand hung limply at his side. It had
been three weeks since the accident and his hand still throbbed
in the cold. Yet he was already back at work because he needed
to make money.

"We have to support our brother workers. If and when we
strike at Putilov, we'll need extra strength from other outside
workers to show we're serious."

"I just don't want to get caught," said Sergei. "Small wages are better than no wages at all."

"Then why are you here?" Lev stopped and faced Sergei. "Why are you part of this movement if you're so afraid?"

"Because I want things to change. I know they need to get better—" He coughed. "But when I read about strikers and what happens to them, I'm not certain we're going to make a difference to management."

"Perhaps our emperor, the Tsar, will see us striking," Lev continued. "And come to our aid. If we can only get our concerns in front of the Tsar, if only he knew about our circumstances, our troubles might be over."

"I'm not so sure that the Tsar..." Sergei hesitated when he saw Lev's expectant face. "But I hope you're right—"

They resumed walking in silence, their heads tilted down slightly, to block the sharp wind and blowing snow. When they were two streets away from the Ekaterinoslav factory, boys and men began to emerge from every direction. Sergei turned his head slowly from side to side, taking in the growing crowd that moved like a flock of animals, steadily forward, growing larger by the minute.

Hundreds of men already waited at the gates to the factory when Sergei and Lev arrived. They were two intense faces among a thousand, each one under a black or brown peaked cap. The factory looked smaller than the Putilov factory, but seemed just as foreboding with its windowless ash-gray exterior, and its tall, cylindrical smokestacks rising up from the roof like canons firing at enemies in the sky.

As the horde continued to grow, Sergei found himself crushed against Lev and a number of strangers. The strong

scent of tobacco mingled with alcohol and bodies made Sergei
wince. Chanting from those closest to the gates began, becoming thunderous as the sky brightened and more voices joined in.

"Eight hours a day," said Sergei, his voice rising gradually
until he shouted, "Eight hours a day."

Beside him, Lev raised his arm and chanted loudly.

After a few minutes, a new chant began from the front of
the crowd, "Minimum wage."

Sergei listened to the men, their voices in unison, calling
for decent wages for all workers. He smiled slightly and added
his strong voice. The chanting continued for more than an hour,
with nobody from inside the factory appearing.

As Sergei took a break to give his throat a rest, he heard the
unmistakable sound of horses coming from behind the strikers.
He suddenly saw a herd of horses with Cossack soldiers gal-
loping directly into the mob. Without warning, the menacing
Cossacks struck right and left with their heavy whips. The strikers in their path were instantly trampled.

Sergei and Lev pushed to their right to get out of the
path of the horses. Sergei thrust his body forward, navigating a
narrow way through the men, screaming for Lev to follow him
closely. He glanced back, saw Lev, and kept pushing through
the flailing men, holding his injured hand up high in the air.
When he reached the edge of the clump of people, he heaved
a sigh of relief. But Lev had disappeared.

He screamed. "Where are you, Lev?" There was no sign
of his friend.

The infantry now joined the Cossacks. Sergei saw a soldier
on foot and moved backward to get out of sight. Shots were
fired. Screams punctured the air. Sergei's shoulders twisted back

as men rushed past him, propelled by fear. The shots got nearer, as did the horses. Sergei began running backwards, straining for a glimpse of Lev. Finally he bolted away, joining the stream of men scattering away from the factory, disappearing into the streets.

Twenty minutes later, when he reached his barracks, Sergei folded over at his waist and breathed heavily, gasping for air.

"What happened to you?" asked Pavel, a beefy man with yellow teeth. He was at least ten years older than Sergei and had a nasty-looking scar across his left cheek from a factory accident.

Sergei stood and then dropped wearily onto his cot. "I went with Lev to strike at Ekaterinoslav, but in the commotion we were—"

Two other workers hurried into the barracks interrupting Sergei. They burst through the door and collapsed on cots about ten feet from Sergei and Pavel.

Sergei got to his feet and moved toward the men. "Did you see Lev?" he asked them.

"Don't know Lev, sorry," said one with bright red hair.

"I didn't see him either," added the other man. "He probably had to run in a different direction to get away. He'll turn up soon."

"Don't go looking for him," said the red-haired man. The police and Cossacks are still rounding up people; if they think you're one of the strikers, you're sure to be picked up."

"Dammit!" said Pavel. "I told Lev not to go to Ekaterinoslav. Too many people were talking about it. I knew the Cossacks would be there. That's why I didn't go."

"You told Lev not to go?" said Sergei.

Pavel nodded grimly.

Sergei sat rigid, his feet on the floor, his injured hand pulsing incessantly.

As the day dragged on, Sergei remained sitting, waiting, listening. Lev never returned. Sergei didn't join his fellow workers for dinner. He waited for Lev. When it came time to go to sleep, Sergei lay down on his back, fully clothed. *I should have made sure Lev was behind me,* he fretted. *I shouldn't have left until I found him. We never should have gone to Ekaterinoslav in the first place. Why didn't Lev listen to Pavel?*

上海

"Where's Lev?" asked the foreman the next morning.

"I'm not sure," said Sergei, lifting his head from the coupling machine. He'd been testing screws with his left hand only, as his other hand still felt sore and stiff.

The foreman gave Sergei a dubious look. "He didn't strike at Ekaterinoslav yesterday, did he?"

"I don't know." With steady eyes, Sergei met the foreman's hard gaze, but inside his stomach lurched. He hated lying, but he couldn't say that Lev had disappeared during the strike. That would imply that he'd also been there. He couldn't let the foreman know that he had become a rebel, a protester, an enemy of his own factory.

The foreman grunted and turned away, but Sergei looked over his shoulder all day long, worried about being watched. Though there were thirteen thousand people working at the Putilov factory, it was well known that those who worked together and lived in the same barracks often became close friends. If the foreman discovered that Lev had been at the strike, he might conclude that Sergei had been there as well, and maybe even that he had joined the Revolutionary Party.

上海

"Eleven strikers were killed and twelve wounded before order was restored at Ekaterinoslav yesterday." Sergei read the first line of the newspaper article three times before continuing. He'd come to the tavern after work with the faint hope that Lev would be sitting there, waiting for him.

"Any news about Lev?" Sergei looked up, saw Pavel, and shook his head. Pavel sat down and set his glass of vodka on the round table. "He could be injured."

"I know. I'm going to check the hospital."

"If he's there, they'll ship him off to Siberia as soon as possible."

Sergei grimaced. "He dreaded the thought of exile more than anything."

"Or he could be dead, which might be better. I'd certainly prefer death over exile or hard labor."

With his good hand, Sergei crumpled the newspaper into a ball and slammed it down on the table. "Dammit! We weren't hurting anybody. We weren't causing trouble. We were just asking for fair wages and hours."

"It's not easy, fighting the wealthy and powerful factory owners who have the support of the Tsar and the police. Combined with the infantry, they outnumber us and have many more weapons," said Pavel. He gestured for another vodka.

The serving girl brought his vodka and set it down. She looked at Sergei, raising her eyebrows to ask if he wanted something. He shook his head and she walked away with a scowl.

"But it's not impossible," Pavel continued. "Remember King Charles the XII of Sweden? He and his army fought and won against Peter the Great, who had an army five times stronger than King Charles's."

"So you think we can force factories to treat us better, even though they have all the power and we have none?"

Pavel sat up straighter. "Surely you don't believe the Revolutionary Party is powerless? Without workers, there are no products, which means factories don't make any money. Factory owners may be able to force the police to come and break up our gatherings, but they also know that if we refuse to work, their factories could go out of business."

"But you didn't strike at Ekaterinoslav," said Sergei. He finished his drink. "If you're so interested in fighting against factory owners, why didn't you go there?"

"I won't be much use to anyone if I'm dead. The Revolutionary Party is no match for the Cossacks' guns and horses." Pavel poured his drink down this throat and wiped his mouth with the back of his hand. "Change will not happen if the Cossacks continue killing our members. We need to outwit them, show the greedy factory owners and the government that represents them that they need us. They're only paying us a pittance but they're making lots of money on what we produce. Only when their profits suffer will they take notice and make changes." He gestured to the serving girl for another drink.

Sergei considered Pavel's words for a moment. "I'm not sure what to think anymore," said Sergei, raising his chin as he spoke. "When we strike, factories cannot operate. Yet we accomplished nothing at Ekaterinoslav. The factory continues to run as usual, and we've lost many good men."

"You're right," said Pavel. The serving girl brought him a full glass of vodka and cleared away the empty one. "There is no clear solution."

"But I don't see any other way to get the factory owners' attention. And Lev lost his freedom, maybe even his life, fighting for better conditions. I'm going to keep striking. For Lev."

"Don't say I didn't warn you." Pavel lifted his glass, gave Sergei a shrug of regret, then tossed the vodka down his throat.

上海

Though Sergei's life had shifted in an instant, with the loss of his friend, the center of Petersburg remained unchanged, as if it were immune to the workers' strife, as if it were a foreign city and not a mere forty-minute-trolley-ride from the factory district.

Sunday afternoon, on his way to the hospital to see if Lev had been admitted, Sergei passed Sir Isaac's Cathedral with its dome soaring into the cold, blue winter sky. People bundled in fur strolled along the sidewalks, their cheeks red from the icy air. Families skated on the Moyka River which meandered gracefully through the city; animated voices rose through the air, penetrating the windows of the trolley. Sergei couldn't believe the vibrancy of the people and the area, compared to the grim mood surrounding the factory. Hard times left no mark on the city.

The snow crunched under Sergei's feet as he made his way along the Nevsky Prospekt. He turned right on the first street past the Moyka River, coming upon the hospital—a large, austere building that towered above neighboring shops and restaurants.

As soon as he entered the doors that led to a bleak white corridor, Sergei recalled his visits to Rachel at the Kishinev Jewish Hospital where he'd encountered the same sterile, medicinal odor, the same hollow stares of people waiting to be seen by doctors, the same subdued cries of misery behind closed doors. He tightened his shoulders and approached the nurse's station.

"May I help you?" asked the nurse, without looking up from her charts. Strands of gray dusted her otherwise brown hair.

"I'm…ummm…trying to find a friend, but I can't remember his last name," said Sergei.

The nurse raised her head, revealing cheeks scarred with divots from smallpox. "Can't be a very good friend if you don't know his full name."

"We worked together."

The nurse tilted her head to one side and appeared to consider Sergei's request. "Name," she said finally.

"Lev. He probably would have come in yesterday."

The nurse flipped through a stack of papers. "We were busier than usual yesterday," she offered, as she glanced at page after page. "With that strike."

Sergei nodded, afraid to say anything that would put him at the strike.

"Nobody by that name has been admitted." She gathered the papers in both hands, and dropped them on her desk until they were neatly contained. "Can't help you. Sorry."

"Thanks for looking." Sergei took one last look at the patients seated around the nurse's station, but did not see Lev.

Lev is either dead or in jail. One day Lev is living and working with me, and the next day, he's gone. Like Mikhail. Like Menahem. Like Rachel. Every time I get close to people, they disappear. From now on, I'm keeping my distance from everyone.

16

Trying to wind down from his troubles, Sergei walked along the Neva River to the Winter Palace, home of the Tsar. He blew on his hands to warm them up and began to sketch the Winter Palace. Since arriving in Petersburg, he'd wanted to draw some of the grand buildings that embellished the city. Now, he yearned to see if he could still sketch buildings and landscapes after his injury at the factory. He moved his wobbly pencil across the paper, but his hand didn't cooperate. His lines looked slanted and unsteady, as if they'd been drawn by a child. Sergei ripped the paper in half and started again.

"Dammit!" he said a moment later, tearing his second drawing out of his sketchbook. "This used to be so easy."

He massaged his aching hand and started a third drawing of the Winter Palace. His fingers grew stiff with cold. He tucked his sketchbook under his arm, rubbed his palms together vigorously, and continued until his fingers froze and refused to move. Sergei kicked a mound of ice and headed back to the barracks.

Once he'd been inside for a while and his hands had warmed up, Sergei continued to draw, from memory, but his fingers still refused to work as they had before his accident. He crumpled his paper and threw it at the doorway, hitting Pavel on the shoulder.

"What the—" Pavel picked up the paper, flattened it, and stared at the image.

"Not bad," said an older man who walked through the doorway and peered at the drawing over Pavel's shoulder.

"I didn't know you could draw," said Pavel.

Sergei jerked his head up. "I can't, not anymore."

"What do you mean? This isn't bad at all," said Pavel.

"I used to be able to draw straight lines at perfect right angles." Sergei said. He flexed his injured hand and frowned. "Now, my sketches look nothing like they're supposed to look. They look more like caricatures."

"This is more interesting than the usual drawings of the Winter Palace," said Pavel. "It reminds me of a poster I saw."

"You know, I think you're right," said the old man.

"A poster?" said Sergei.

"A tobacco poster," said Pavel, sidling towards Sergei. "The way you've drawn the people in front of the building." He looked squarely at Sergei. "You know, you might be able to draw some posters for the Revolutionary Party. We could use more people and your drawing could work as an advertisement for new members. You'd have a far bigger impact creating a poster for the cause than by striking. And you'd be paid."

"I had planned to be an architect one day," said Sergei. "It never occurred to me that my sketches might be used for a revolution."

Pavel handed the paper to Sergei and crossed his arms. "A peaceful revolution. We're only asking for what we deserve. Besides, working with faulty machinery is what injured your hand. If you ask me, it's fate."

Sergei studied his drawing and sighed. "I promised my mother I'd do everything I could to become an architect."

"Promises are made to be broken," said Pavel. "Besides, you'd be well-paid for your time. I'm sure your mother would not disapprove of her son making decent money."

"Maybe my hand will improve," Sergei mused, glancing at his hand. "Maybe I'll still be able to become an architect."

"Right," scoffed Pavel. "And maybe they'll start paying us better tomorrow."

上海

Very early the next morning before work, Sergei took another walk toward the Winter Palace, thinking about his new prospects. It was February 9. He'd been in Petersburg ten months and had saved nothing for university. Sergei hoped Pavel was telling him the truth, that by drawing posters for the Revolutionary Party, he'd make enough money to send home and have some extra for school. As he threaded his way under the General Staff Arch, Sergei could see an ebullient crowd gathering at the Palace Square in front of the Winter Palace. The sprawling creamy-yellow General Staff Building seemed to be watching over everyone, with its three storeys of windows looking down upon the congested square. In the center, the Alexander I Column rose triumphantly, marking Russia's defeat of Napolean in 1812.

He stopped when he saw a procession headed toward the square. Thousands of people, their faces cheery despite the frigid air, gazed in the direction of the Winter Palace, as if expecting the Tsar to appear. Students, carrying banners that said, "Long live the Tsar," and "Victory is ours," stood with their heads held high, singing hymns of praise.

"What's going on?" Sergei asked a ruddy-looking man with a child atop his shoulders.

"Japan attacked the Russian squadron in Lushunkou, Port Arthur, last night," said the man. Smoky tendrils emerged from his mouth as his warm breath met the cold air.

From what he'd read in the newspaper, Sergei knew that Port Arthur, on the southern tip of Manchuria, was a year-round port that opened to the Yellow Sea and the Pacific Ocean. A few years earlier, Russia had negotiated with China a twenty-five-year lease for the use of Port Arthur. Now the Tsar wanted total control over this ice-free port so he could trade with other countries during the winter. On the other side, the Japanese wanted a well-fortified barrier to protect their own independence. They believed Port Arthur was theirs after a hard-won victory over China during the Sino-Japanese War that ended in 1895.

"The Japanese are fools. We've got three million men to their six hundred thousand," offered another man. "Victory will be ours in a matter of days."

The ruddy-looking man lifted his child off his shoulders and set her down. "Winning Port Arthur is good for Russian trade, good for all of us."

That's why people are here? thought Sergei. *To celebrate the war? Hasn't there been enough killing of Russian people?*

The man nodded and took his daughter's hand. "We're

here to thank the Tsar for looking out for his people. If we get an ice-free port, we can trade all winter. Things are bound to improve for all of us."

The crowd's murmur increased to a roar. Sergei peered ahead at the three arched doors and saw the middle one open. The red-bearded Tsar Nicholas II appeared, a commanding figure amidst the opulence of his palace. He raised his arm in a salute but said nothing. No words were necessary, for the crowd's voices increased in unison, as if cued by a conductor. Even when the Tsar withdrew, seconds after his salute, the excitement continued to rise.

Sergei scanned the faces surrounding him, taken aback by the awe most Russians held for the Tsar, a reverence for the emperor that went back generations. But now, the Tsar and his henchmen had crushed Lev and injured and killed many other strikers.

Sergei tried to step back against the wave of people pushing forward. The farther he moved from the Tsar's fervent supporters, the more separate he felt from his own people, like a fox without a home.

17

When the laundry's bell rang, bringing the working day to a close, Rachel told Shprintze and Anna she had to go to pick up a few things at the market and wouldn't be able to go home with them. They gave her a long, hard stare that made Rachel squirm. She knew that her friends could see through her words.

"I suppose I don't have to get them today," Rachel said.

"No, you should take a break before supper." Shprintze wrapped her shawl tightly around her neck and shoulders, held her head high, and waddled out of the laundry. Shprintze's belly was so swollen that Rachel wondered if there were two babies inside.

Rachel craved some time alone, a rarity living in such a small room with her sister and Menahem. She strode briskly out of the laundry and headed down the street. It had been fourteen hours since she'd begun working, a typical day for her. Every day

seemed longer with a never-ending stream of dirty clothing and
bedding. Her swollen fingers ached, and her back felt so stiff
she feared she'd never be able to stand upright again. Worst of
all…the futility of what she did six days a week, the mindless-
ness of washing clothes when she wanted to be in school, to
have the time to read and write. Even her journal had suffered
because she was always too tired, and her hands were too sore
for writing.

This can't be all there is to my life. She stopped and watched a
group of children rolling down the bank of the Huangpu River.
Only a couple of years ago, she had enjoyed springtime, just like
these children, with no worries or fears.

Keeping her quick pace, Rachel strode past a Jewish furrier,
a bank, a bakery, and a crowded restaurant. In the International
Settlement, it seemed hard to believe she was in Shanghai. All
the shops were run by people who'd come from other countries,
signs and advertisements were in every language except Chinese,
and Chinese people were rarely seen. At the opposite end of
Nanking Road, Rachel came upon the place she'd been looking
for: a Yiddish shop—Pressman Books. At the very back of the
shop stood four shelves stuffed with Yiddish books, magazines,
and newspapers, including *Der fraynd (The Friend)*, the Yiddish
newspaper published in Petersburg that had been her father's
favorite.

She pulled the glass door open and smiled at the owner, Mr.
Pressman, a round-faced man with frizzy long hair who never
minded Rachel coming in to read without buying anything. He
nodded at Rachel and turned back to his customer, a woman
buying a couple of books and some magazines. Rachel marched
purposefully to the back of the store and ran her fingers across

the spines of the books. She pulled a thick volume from the shelf, an anthology of Yiddish literature. Rachel sat down on the hard, wood floor and read a story, stopping at one point to re-read a thought-provoking passage.

"How are you today, Miss Paskar?"

Mr. Pressman's voice startled Rachel, causing her to drop the book.

He bent down, onto one knee, and picked up the book. "Good choice," he said, studying the cover. "A very good choice."

"I'm sorry I dropped it." Rachel stumbled to her feet and smoothed her skirt with her hands.

"No harm done." Mr. Pressman stood and held the book out to her.

"I really should be going."

Mr. Pressman shrugged and put the book back on the shelf.

Rachel moved reluctantly toward the front of the store. On the sidewalk outside the shop, a group of Chinese men promenaded by, their dark eyes focused straight ahead. "I hardly ever see Chinese people in this district," she said.

"I've been here two years and know very little about them," said Mr. Pressman. "One fellow I know is learning their language, but still finds it difficult to engage Chinese people in conversation. One of the few things he's learned is that the gate of the old city facing the water is called Gate of the Peaceful Sea."

"That's beautiful. I wish I could speak Chinese. I want to know how to read their intricate alphabet. I want to know what they eat, what they believe in, what they read."

Mr. Pressman chuckled. "Your curiosity is a true gift, and, I daresay, the sign of a future writer?"

"I have written one article for the *Israel's Messenger*, but haven't had time to do another."

"You should make time for something so important." Mr. Pressman smiled fondly at Rachel and folded his arms across his chest.

Rachel twirled her braid. "I'll try."

"Don't be a stranger," called out Mr. Pressman.

"I won't." Rachel stepped outside. The sun hung low in the sky and a few drops of rain landed on her nose. She tilted her face upward, but no more drops fell.

上海

Rachel and Shprintze sat across from one another at the dining table, the first ones to arrive for the Sabbath meal.

"What does it feel like, having a baby inside you?" asked Rachel.

Shprintze examined her abdomen and rubbed it affectionately. "Like my heart is bigger. It seems almost magical how my body is creating another." She smiled shyly. "Do you want to feel?"

Rachel stood and moved around to Shprintze. She put her hand over Shprintze's stomach but did not touch her.

"You have to have your hand on my belly to feel the baby." Shprintze took Rachel's hand and laid it over the bulge in her abdomen.

For a second nothing happened. Then a tiny yet forceful jab made Rachel jump.

"I felt him kick!" she cried. "He's really in there."

"Of course he is." Sadness flickered in her eyes. "I just wish we had a home."

Rachel removed her hand and sat down beside Shprintze. "You will someday."

The door from the street opened and Anna appeared, with a crumpled letter in her hand and a stricken expression. "I just got a letter from my husband. A Russian battleship struck three Japanese mines at Port Arthur and exploded. More than six hundred men were killed." Anna's freckles looked more prominent than usual against her wan skin.

"How can Russia keep going, with losses like that?" responded Rachel.

"That is what I wonder every day. But when I read the newspaper and see how many men are fighting and how many have been wounded and killed, I fear it will never end," said Anna choking back tears. "I fear for my husband's life."

She sat on the bench beside Rachel, who gave Anna a reassuring pat on the back. But Rachel, too, was distraught—and angry.

"Your husband should try and escape from the army," said Rachel. "The Russian government is drafting more Jews than ever. Yet they're treated so poorly. I can't imagine why any Jew would willingly fight in a war that is not ours, for a country that banishes us to the Pale, for people who treat us like parasites."

"I know," said Anna. "But deserting is not the answer. Six Jewish soldiers who tried to flee the army were shot to death by Russian soldiers a few days ago. My husband must stay."

The other tenants began arriving for Sabbath dinner. Once everyone sat down, Danka Muller lit two white candles in the middle of the table. Rachel tried to get into the peaceful spirit of the Sabbath but it was difficult for her. *I sometimes hate the quiet of the Sabbath*, she thought. She gazed at the flames, dancing on the tops of the candles. She tried to put aside her frustration with her job, her resentment toward the laundry manager who was never satisfied with her work. She tried to forget about the war in Port Arthur and the possibility of Anna being left a widow. And, most of all, she could not stop thinking about her mother, alone and ill, and waiting to die.

Mr. Muller recited the *kiddish*, the blessing over the wine, and everyone around the table exchanged greetings.

"*Gut shabes*," said Menahem in Yiddish, to Rachel.

Rachel forced a smile for Menahem's sake. "*A gut yor*," she replied.

Across the table, Jacob said, "*Shabat shalom*," in Hebrew and exchanged a private smile with Nucia.

Yehiel Mendelssohn said a blessing over the challah and then the simple meal began. Rachel broke off a piece of challah and put it in her mouth. The warm bread formed a knot in her throat that was difficult to swallow.

"I have decided to join the army in Port Arthur," announced Yosef Trumpeldor. He pounded the table with his fist.

Gasps of dismay were heard around the table. Rachel choked on her bread.

"Are you crazy?" Rachel asked Yosef. "Every day I read about Jewish soldiers hurt or killed in this war which has nothing to do with us."

"We were born in Russia. It is the country of our ancestors," said Yosef. "How can you even think this war will not affect us?"

"We have been forced out of Russia like pests, and have lost everything because of our faith," she answered. "How will winning an ice-free port help us?"

"It's not just about the port. It's about proving our loyalty to Russia. It's about protecting the country where many of our relatives still live. After serving, I will be able to settle down outside the Pale. I will have opportunities never seen by Jews before. And I will be able to raise my children in their own country with pride. Nobody will call me or my family cowards or deserters."

"It's easy for you to speak so boldly, when you haven't spent a night in the army. You've never been separated from the Russian men, treated as an inferior person just because you are a Jew. You should read my husband's letters," exclaimed Anna.

"Your loyalty is commendable, Yosef," said Yehiel Mendelssohn. "But you must be prepared for discrimination, no matter how bravely you fight."

"True," admitted Yosef, "but I'm confident that Russian commanders will appreciate my patriotism and my value as a soldier."

"You're wrong," said Rachel. "They'll never see you as anything but a pesky Jew. Are you really willing to risk your life for equality, something we've been trying to attain for hundreds of years without success?"

"You're only a girl. What do you know?" answered Yosef, dismissively. "I have made my decision and will be leaving for Port Arthur on the next ship." He strode away from the table without eating anything on his plate.

Nobody uttered a word during the remainder of the meal.

上海

The friends from the hostel took a walk near the banks of the Huangpu River on a Sunday afternoon. It had been two weeks since Yosef Trumpeldor had announced his intention to fight for the Russian army, and he'd already departed for Port Arthur.

"I think I need to rest for a moment," said Shprintze, lowering her top-heavy frame onto the ground beneath a walnut tree.

"Are you all right?" asked Isaac. He sat beside his wife and draped his arm over her shoulders.

Shprintze leaned back and rested her weight on the tree's broad trunk. "I'm just happy to be out of my room."

Rachel watched Nucia and Jacob strolling along the river about a hundred feet away, on their way to see the ships in the harbor. Jacob had Menahem on his shoulders, and from behind, they looked like father and son.

"I still can't believe Yosef went back to Russia," said Anna, breaking the comfortable silence. "I wish he and my husband could have traded places."

"Yosef is the most foolish man I've ever met," said Rachel. "He was lucky enough to make it to Shanghai, to be educated as a dentist, yet he throws it all away like a stone in the river!"

"He's going to regret his decision when he faces the Japanese," said Isaac. "Especially now when morale is so low. The Russian naval commander was killed when his ship was sunk by a mine last week. Six hundred thirty-five Russian soldiers died in the explosion."

"My husband sounded miserable in the letter I received yesterday," said Anna. She gazed at the river. "The Japanese attacked his unit. But thankfully he survived."

"Will you read it to us?" asked Isaac.

Anna looked at him gratefully, as if she'd been hoping he'd ask. She smoothed out the letter and began in a shaky voice:

A couple of weeks ago, my unit saw a little spot on the horizon, and then another and another, until there were fifteen spots. As we drew nearer, we saw a tiny puff of smoke, a projectile launched at Port Arthur. We had no idea where it would fall and rushed to find a safe place to hide. Forty fathoms below the cliff where we were stationed, lay the battleship Peresviet. We heard a big bang and a shell burst under her bows. Another puff and a projectile whistled overhead, crashing on the rocks behind us. A third puff and then a terrific explosion over our heads. We opened fire and the sea almost boiled with the swish and plunge of projectiles. The smoke and dust blinded me, but I wasn't hurt.

"That's a relief," exclaimed Rachel.

"But I'm very frightened for my husband," said Anna. "Every day I imagine him walking through the hostel door with that big silly grin of his. And every day I'm disappointed."

Menahem's laughter from above Jacob's shoulders interrupted them. Rachel turned and saw Menahem, Nucia, and Jacob coming toward them. Jacob set Menahem down and the boy raced toward Rachel.

"Were there many ships?" Rachel asked Menahem.

"More than I've ever seen," he answered excitedly. He nestled against Rachel.

"Menahem is fascinated by the sails," said Jacob, sitting

near Rachel, pulling Nucia down beside him. "I think he'd like to captain a ship one day."

Rachel chuckled and tousled Menahem's hair affectionately.

"Can we go to the harbor again tomorrow?" asked Menahem.

"I have to work tomorrow," answered Nucia. "If I get home in time."

Rachel didn't even bother to respond. She worked much longer hours at the laundry than Nucia for the same pay, because she was not a skilled seamstress like her sister. She never got home before dark. Rachel pulled Menahem closer and felt his heart beating.

"What do you think Sergei is doing right now?" he asked Rachel.

"Well, he is probably resting so that he can be awake in the factory tomorrow," she stammered.

Menahem said nothing for a moment. "I miss him."

Rachel saw Jacob take Nucia's hand and hold it tight. "So do I," she said softly.

18

U nder candlelight, Rachel wrote in her journal while Nucia and Menahem slept. Rachel liked being the only person awake, having the night to herself.

A knock at the door startled Rachel. She dropped her feather pen and jumped up to get to the door before another knock woke her sister or Menahem. Isaac stood in the corridor, his face gray with worry.

"It's coming," he said. "The baby's coming."

"I'll go fetch the doctor," said Nucia, awakened by Isaac's voice. She hurriedly put on her dress and ran out of the room.

"What's happening?" asked Menahem groggily.

"Shprintze is going to have her baby tonight," said Rachel. "I'm going to be with her in her room. You stay here."

Menahem, now fully awake, nodded, sat up in his cot, and pulled his knees to his chest.

Rachel followed Isaac to his room where Shprintze's groans could clearly be heard through the thin walls.

"I'm so scared, Rachel," said Shprintze when she saw Rachel.

"You will be fine, I'm sure of it." Rachel turned to Isaac who stood shaking. "Fill the basin with warm water and fetch some clean cloths," she said.

Isaac hurried from the room with the empty basin.

"How do you know what to do?" asked Shprintze.

Before Rachel could answer, Shprintze cried out and clutched her abdomen. Rachel rubbed Shprintze's head and stared at the doorway. *Where is the doctor? What if Nucia can't find him?*

"There were many babies born in the houses near mine in Kishinev," said Rachel, keeping one eye on the door and one eye on Shprintze. "I know that basins of water and many cloths were needed."

"Oh!" Shprintze's body twisted and she screamed out sharply. "It hurts, please help me…"

Rachel covered her own mouth to keep from crying out and stared at the closed door, willing it to open with the doctor. Shprintze grabbed Rachel's forearm and gripped it so tightly that her skin turned white and went numb.

Rachel glanced at the motionless door again. "Imagine you're in a beautiful meadow filled with flowers—chamomiles as yellow as the sun, pink roses, tall lilies—"

"Lilies…are my…favorite," grunted Shprintze.

"Good, that's good. Think of yourself lying in a field of lilies, smell them, touch them."

Shprintze squeezed her eyes shut. The strain on her friend's face terrified Rachel, who began to worry that something was wrong, that she should be doing more for Shprintze.

The piercing screeches from Shprintze became quicker and louder.

"You're doing well," said Rachel in a soothing voice.

The door opened and Isaac ran to Rachel, the water in the basin slopping from side to side as he moved. He set the basin down on the floor near Rachel and handed her a brown cloth. Rachel dipped it in the cool water and placed it on Shprintze's brow. "Soon you're going to be holding your baby, very soon."

Isaac paced back and forth, his hands clasped as if in prayer.

The door burst open five minutes later and the doctor strode in. Rachel almost wept in relief. Nucia hovered in the doorway with a skittish Danka Muller. Isaac collapsed in a heap on the floor.

"What have we here?" asked the doctor, a young Polish man with neatly trimmed whiskers. He pulled out a pocket watch with one hand, and measured Shprintze's pulse with his other.

Nucia introduced him as Dr. Goldszmit.

Shprintze, her face bathed in sweat, hardly noticed the doctor. She cried out, still gripping Rachel's arm.

"Just my luck," the doctor muttered. "I drag myself out of bed only to find I'm not needed here." He winked at Rachel. "You seem to have everything under control. I don't think you really need me."

"Don't go," pleaded Rachel. "We can't deliver a baby by ourselves."

Dr. Goldszmit grinned and washed his hands in the basin.

"I. Can't do. This," grunted Shprintze. "I'm not. Ready."

The doctor pushed his white sleeves up to his elbows and positioned himself at Shprintze's feet. "You may not be ready, but your baby is. Now, the next time you feel a pain in your belly, push as hard as you can."

Shprintze looked at Rachel, who squeezed her hand.

"Oh, here it comes," shouted Shprintze. Her eyes were glassy as she stared at the wall and pushed.

"Well done," said Dr. Goldszmit. "Now, every time you feel the pain, push, and before you know it, you'll have your baby."

"How long?" asked Rachel. She tried to wipe the sweat off Shprintze's brow, but as soon as she did, more arose from her pores.

The doctor looked at his watch. "Could be a few minutes, could be a few hours."

Rachel pasted a smile on her lips, and told Shprintze that everything would be fine now.

For hours, until dawn, Shprintze pushed with a strength that astonished and terrified Rachel. Then, when Rachel began to think Shprintze didn't really have a baby inside of her, the doctor declared that it was a girl. A shrill cry followed.

"A girl, a baby girl," echoed Rachel.

"Isaac wanted a girl," murmured Shprintze. Her voice sounded weak. She closed her eyes and lay still for the first time in hours.

Rachel could not stop staring at the tiny, fragile baby girl as the doctor wiped the blood and milky-white liquid from her. The baby opened her mouth and cried again, producing a wonderful sound, the sound of new life, the sound of hope. Rachel helped the doctor swaddle the baby in a clean sheet and, smiling with gratitude, handed her to Shprintze.

"Hello, Zelda," whispered Shprintze, gazing into her baby's eyes.

"That's a beautiful name," said Rachel.

"It was Isaac's mother's name," said Shprintze, without taking her eyes off Zelda.

Naming a baby after a deceased relative was a common Jewish tradition.

Rachel watched baby Zelda's eyes focus on Shprintze and decided that this was one of her favorite traditions because it honored the past and ensured people would never be forgotten.

上海

A day after Zelda was born, Yehiel Mendelssohn made an announcement over dinner at the hostel. "I received a letter from Yosef Trumpeldor," he said. "He lost an arm during an attack against a Japanese squadron."

Rachel froze, holding her bread in mid-air. The sound of rain showering the hostel grew louder as all conversations stopped abruptly.

"Oh my goodness," exclaimed Danka Muller, bringing her hand over her mouth. "That's horrible."

"Is he coming back to Shanghai?" asked Jacob. He rubbed his shoulder as if he needed to reassure himself that it was still there, still attached to his body.

"Excuse me," said Anna, standing up. Her face had turned as white as the challah. She ran upstairs.

"He wants to keep fighting," said Yehiel Mendelssohn. "He might even be back at the front now."

"But that's crazy," said Rachel. "How can he fight with one arm? He's going to get himself killed."

"In his letter, Yosef wrote that the Russians lost three

thousand men in one week, all eight of their machine guns and eleven field guns," continued Yehiel Mendelssohn. "He says the Japanese are proving to be a much stronger opponent than anybody imagined, so he must stay and keep fighting."

"He's already sacrificed enough for a country that considers us to be vermin," said Rachel.

"What if Yosef loses his other arm?" asked Menahem, his face shadowed with concern. "How will he eat?"

"I think we have talked enough about Yosef," said Rachel, looking around the table. She turned to Menahem. "I'm sure Yosef will be fine if he feels well enough to stay in Port Arthur."

As soon as she finished eating, Rachel went upstairs to see if Anna needed anything, or wanted to talk. She tapped Anna's door lightly. "It's me, Rachel," she said. "Can I come in?"

No response. Rachel pressed her ear against the door. "Anna?"

Nothing. "Just because Yosef is injured, doesn't mean the same thing will happen to your husband."

"I know," Anna replied in a thin voice. "I just want to be by myself right now."

Rachel stood outside Anna's door for a couple of minutes, to make sure she didn't change her mind about wanting to talk. When no further sound came from inside Anna's room, Rachel went into her own room and tried to write in her journal. But the sound of the rain pounding at the window, and the thought of missing an arm distracted her. After an hour, she hadn't written a word.

19

The rain continued for seven days and nights, saturating the air with dampness. Even the laundry contained a chill that made it difficult to dry the wet garments. The worst part of the rain, thought Rachel, as she moved an iron back and forth over a red tablecloth, was that she couldn't get to the medical building easily tonight. In the many months that they had been in Shanghai, she visited the building regularly, even though she couldn't get into the quarantined area to see her mother. Even being outside the building where her mother lay ill, somehow eased her longing, calmed her spirit.

The iron stuck to the fabric and a burning smell rose through the air. Rachel yanked the iron from the fabric. A black spot, the exact shape and size of the iron, remained on the linen. The fabric had still been damp when she'd started ironing, causing the iron to stick to it. Rachel gathered the tablecloth in her arms and shoved it under the table.

When the bell announced the end of the work day, Rachel waited until the manager had gone to the back of the room, and dashed out of the laundry with the ruined tablecloth bundled in her arms.

"What if he realizes a tablecloth is missing?" asked Anna.

"We get hundreds of tablecloths like that for restaurants," said Rachel. "He never counts them."

"Maybe you should have told him. I'm sure he would understand one mistake."

"I don't think so. Remember how he fired that woman a few weeks ago, for being late because her baby had been sick all night?"

That night, just after midnight, the rain stopped. Rachel, who had not fallen asleep, leapt from her cot to the window. Wet patches in the alley reflected like murky pools under the full moon. She opened the window and stuck her head out to see if the rain had really ended. The heavy scent of rain lingered, but the air seemed clear.

"What are you doing, Rachel?" asked Menahem in a groggy voice.

"The rain's gone!" she cried, her voice louder than she intended.

"Go back to sleep," mumbled Nucia, half-awake.

Rachel left the window open and crawled back in beside Menahem. She rolled from side to side but could not get comfortable. Down the hall a baby cried out…Shprintze's baby wanted to be fed. Outside, a horse-drawn carriage sped past, making splashing sounds as it moved through puddles.

Tomorrow, I will try to see Mother, vowed Rachel. She pictured the building, the guard outside the door, the fence that kept sick people in and healthy people out. She knew every inch by heart, she'd been at the door so many times. But wait... Rachel sat upright. There were no guards at night. And one small section of the wall, at the back of the building, used for deliveries, stood only about four feet high.

"Menahem, wake up." Rachel prodded his shoulder with her hand.

He lifted his head, then dropped it down.

"We're going to see Mother," Rachel whispered.

Menahem raised his head again. "Mother Ita?"

Rachel nodded. "I think I know a way to get in, to actually see her."

Menahem squinted. "Is it morning already?"

"No, that's why we have to go now, when the guards are gone."

"What are you doing?" asked Nucia, her voice coarse with sleep.

"Going to see Mother. Get up. Hurry," urged Rachel. She buttoned the waist of her brown skirt.

"Sometimes I think you truly are crazy," said Nucia. "You've tried to get in to see her every week since we've been here, only to be sent away each time. What makes you think you can break in during the middle of the night and find her?"

"I don't have time to explain," answered Rachel, pulling on her felt boots. "Just trust me."

Nucia gave her a dubious look and sighed. She got out of her cot, dressed quickly in a long skirt and blouse, and followed Rachel and Menahem out of the room.

Every creak on the staircase sounded louder than usual to Rachel as she led the way down. The three of them scurried off to the medical building. Moonlight lit the way, as if it wanted to lead them right to their mother. Fifteen minutes later, the white medical center loomed in front of them like a church—mysterious and intimidating.

"This is a bad idea," said Nucia, her gaze fixed on the building. "We should go back before anyone sees us."

"I'm not leaving until I see Mother." Rachel marched past the front gate along the side of the building with Menahem at her heels.

Nucia puckered her lips, looked at Rachel, then at the building, and rushed to catch up.

Rachel wrapped her hands around the delivery gate at the back of the building. It faced the harbor which lay serenely under the night sky. "You climb onto my shoulders, Menahem, and pull yourself over the fence."

She bent down and rested her palms on her knees. Menahem scrambled onto her back and encircled her neck with his arms. Rachel stood and pushed Menahem gently until his feet were on her shoulders. She held onto the gate to balance herself and keep from falling over.

"What if he gets hurt?" cried Nucia, her hands around her mouth.

"He'll be fine," said Rachel.

Menahem's foot pressed sharply into her shoulder as he used her to leverage himself over the fence. He swung his legs over and dropped onto the ground on the other side.

"You go now," said Rachel to Nucia.

Nucia, her face rigid with apprehension, hoisted her right leg over the railing. She jumped on her left leg and tried to haul herself over but made no progress. Rachel picked up her sister's left foot and lifted until Nucia dangled precariously on the railing, her long skirt bunched up to her waist. She tried to pull it down to cover her bare legs.

"Don't worry about your skirt," said Rachel. "Just let yourself fall to the right."

Nucia opened her mouth and shrieked as she fell over the railing, landing on her bottom.

"Sh!" Rachel peered around to see if anyone had heard Nucia and come to investigate. Nobody appeared. She lifted her right leg but couldn't reach the top of the railing. She bent her left knee and hopped, hurdling her right leg over, getting stuck in the middle like Nucia. The railing pressed uncomfortably into her abdomen.

Nucia and Menahem chuckled at the sight of Rachel straddling the gate.

"You looked exactly like me, Nucia," said Rachel.

"True, but it's much more amusing seeing you stuck like that."

Rachel took a deep breath and swung her left leg over, landing on her hands and bottom. Her hands skidded across the ground, slicing her skin open. She looked at her bleeding hands and grimaced.

"That looks painful," said Nucia.

"I'll be fine." Rachel got to her feet and ignored the burning sensation on her hands.

"What do we do now?" asked Menahem.

Rachel shoved aside a wooden cart on wheels and examined a shaft that opened into the cart. She stood under the shaft which enclosed her to her waist and said something indecipherable, her voice echoing inside the shaft.

"What?" said Nucia.

Rachel poked her head out from under the shaft. "We're going to crawl up the laundry chute."

"Oh, no," protested Nucia. "There is no way I can make it up there."

"You've come this far," said Rachel. "You can't back down now."

Nucia shook her head.

"Menahem will go first, then you, and I'll go last so I can help," offered Rachel.

"You can do it, Nucia," said Menahem.

"It's the only way in, the only way we can see Mother," added Rachel.

"But you don't even know where she is in this place," said Nucia. "What if we climb through here and then get caught?"

"She has to be on the second floor. When we first came here, they kept us on the first floor, remember? To segregate sick people, they have to keep them on another floor," said Rachel.

"But what if someone sees us?" Nucia asked.

"Are they going to put us in jail for trying to see our own mother?" said Rachel.

Nucia tilted her head back and looked at the sky. "How did I let myself be talked into such a crazy scheme?"

Rachel hoisted Menahem into the shaft. The sound of his feet against the sides of the chute subsided as he moved further along.

"Your turn," said Rachel to Nucia.

"Ugh." Nucia positioned herself under the shaft and pulled herself up.

As soon as Nucia had gone a few feet, Rachel climbed in and lugged herself up using her forearms and feet for traction. Luckily, the chute sloped upward gently, making it easy to move forward. Up ahead, she heard Menahem and Nucia progressing steadily to the second floor, their feet banging against the side of the chute.

It took approximately ten minutes to reach the top of the chute, where each of them squeezed through a swinging door into the hospital laundry. White linen had been piled neatly on wide tables; the room looked spotless, even the white floors gleamed. There were no windows, only one small door.

"Come on." Rachel gestured for Nucia and Menahem to follow her through the door. She put her finger in front of her lips.

The corridor seemed eerily quiet and dark. Moonlight streamed through the window on their left; on the right, the corridor opened up to a large, well-lit vestibule about twenty feet from them. Doors, marked with names of patients, lined both sides of the hall. Squinting, Rachel read the names on the first door and shook her head. She continued moving toward the window, with Nucia and Menahem close behind. At the room at the end of the hall, beside the window, Rachel read the names silently, then out loud with reverence. "Ita Paskar."

Nucia, standing behind her sister, clutched Rachel's elbow. "Mother. We found her."

Menahem opened the door and ran inside, stopping abruptly when he saw four identical beds on two walls, with patients' feet facing the center of the room. "Mother Ita?" Menahem shrank back and looked up at Rachel with eyes as big as kopecks.

The small, rectangular room teemed with the smell of sickness and neglect. A curtain had been drawn over the only window, obstructing the outside world. Rachel walked down the middle of the room, examining every sleeping woman. One snored so loudly, Rachel couldn't believe she didn't wake herself up. Another rolled fitfully from side to side, moaning in her sleep, as if she were having a bad dream. Rachel stopped at the last bed on the right, and motioned for Menahem and Nucia to join her. In the bed lay her mother, so thin, the blanket barely rose above the mattress. Her breathing sounded belabored, raspy, much like it had been on their journey to Shanghai, only weaker. The struggle for air seemed to take all of her energy.

Rachel opened the curtain, bathing the room in soft moonlight. Her mother's head turned slowly toward the window revealing her emaciated face. It looked as if her skin had been stretched across her bones. And broken blood vessels crisscrossed her cheeks like woven fishnets.

"You're here," said Rachel's mother haltingly. The strain of talking took her breath away. Her hair, once lustrous and abundant, now looked thin with bare spots on her scalp. Rachel took her mother's hand. It too seemed to have shrunk and felt cold. "We've been so worried about you."

"We miss you," said Nucia. She kissed her mother's forehead.

Rachel wanted to hold her mother close, but feared she'd break her fragile bones.

"And here's our Menahem," croaked her mother, reaching out for the boy.

Menahem moved in closer, between Nucia and Rachel. He sobbed and dropped his head onto Mother Ita's chest.

Rachel tightened her grasp on her mother's hand. "I've tried to see you so many times, but they never let me in."

"I know," said her mother with a feeble smile. "The doctors have told me."

Rachel bit her lip.

"You don't have to talk, Mother," said Nucia.

Menahem lifted his head and sniffed loudly. "When are you going to get better?"

Anguish darkened Mother Ita's ashen face. She tried to change the subject, "Tell me about Shanghai."

Rachel and Nucia exchanged solemn looks.

"It rains all the time," said Menahem. "And it smells bad."

"But the people are nice," said Rachel, "especially the ones at our hostel."

"We're working hard," said Nucia, "and Menahem goes to a good Jewish school."

Their mother nodded with pleasure.

"School's not that interesting," said Menahem. "I like watching the boats and swimming with Jacob more."

"Jacob?" said their mother.

Nucia blushed. "He lives at the hostel. I have been seeing him a little."

"She sees him every day," said Rachel. "He is good to Nucia and treats Menahem well."

"I am happy to hear this."

"I hope they get married," said Menahem. "So Jacob will stay with us and not leave."

Rachel wrapped her arm around Menahem.

"Rachel has written for the newspaper," said Nucia. "And they pay her."

A lump in her mother's throat rose and fell. "Your father would be very proud."

"She's very talented," added Nucia.

"Someday you will write in America," said their mother to Rachel.

"You will be with us, to see my words in print," said Rachel.

"No. Sadly my days will end here."

"Don't say that, Mother," cried Rachel. "You will get better. You need to eat more, to gain your strength. Remember? That's what you always told us when we were sick."

"What's going on?" interrupted a woman's sharp voice.

A nurse stood in the doorway, astonishment written all over her face. "How did you get in here?"

"You must go," said their mother.

"Who is it?" said another patient in the room, awakened by the commotion.

"I can't leave you here, not like this," said Rachel to her mother.

"Don't worry. They take good care of me here." She gently pulled her hand from Rachel's.

"This is against our rules. I'm getting the doctor and the police," said the nurse. She marched down the hall, her arms bent at the elbows in determination.

"We have to go," said Nucia, kissing her mother's forehead again. "Before they throw us in jail."

"We haven't done anything wrong," said Rachel.

"Now is not the time to debate." Nucia grabbed Menahem's hand and dragged him to the doorway.

"Goodbye, Mother Ita," cried Menahem.

"I will come back," promised Rachel. She kissed her mother's cheek and backed away from her.

"No," said her mother. "Just remember me as I was in Kishinev."

"Don't talk like that," said Rachel.

"I am ready for *Gan-eyden,* the Garden of Eden."

Rachel pressed her lips together, gave her mother one last look, and hurried down the hall.

Numb right to her bones, Rachel followed her sister and Menahem down the chute, her head bent in grief. Driven by fear, they climbed over the fence much faster than they had coming in, and ran until they were a good distance from the medical building. A grave silence came over them as they walked the rest of the way back to the hostel. Then they climbed into their cots and waited for morning.

上海

Four nights after seeing her mother, Rachel woke suddenly with an excruciating pain in her gut. She could barely breathe.

Menahem moaned in his sleep. One of his eyes opened, stared blearily at Rachel, then closed again.

Rachel lay still, gripped by a sense of panic that grew stronger by the minute. When the first light streamed through the window, she rose silently, dressed, and left the hostel. She headed directly toward the medical building and stood outside the gate. The thought that she should be at work crossed her mind, but she knew without a doubt that she needed to be here.

She didn't have long to wait. Before the sun climbed much

higher in the sky, the doctor emerged from the medical building. He moved toward Rachel as if he'd been expecting her. Close up, he looked as if he hadn't slept in weeks.

"How did you know?" he asked her.

"You mean…she's gone?"

"Yes. About an hour ago."

"Oh no!" Rachel slumped onto the ground.

"She looked very peaceful, glad to be out of pain," the doctor continued. "I think seeing you one last time freed her to go."

"You heard about our visit?"

The doctor chuckled. "It's all anyone is talking about around here."

Rachel gave him a rueful smile.

"How on earth did you get in?"

Rachel opened her mouth to answer.

The doctor put his hand up. "No, don't tell me. The less I know, the better."

Rachel rubbed her throbbing temple.

"You can have the funeral at the Jewish cemetery if you like," the doctor continued.

Rachel couldn't speak.

"I can have it arranged for sunset, tonight…"

It seemed unreal to Rachel. How could it be possible that her mother, once a strong, healthy woman, needed a funeral?

"Does that work for you and the rest of your family, tonight?"

Rachel nodded mutely.

"At the Israelite Cemetery, on Mohawk Road."

Rachel continued to nod.

"I will meet you there at six, with your mother's body."

Rachel's eyes glazed over.

"Are you going to be all right?" asked the doctor. "Do you want someone to walk back with you?"

"No, I'll manage myself." Rachel ran back toward the hostel. When, out of breath, she came to the Hongkew Creek, she knelt down and put her hands in the cool, muddy water. She cupped her fingers and held them over her face so that the water drenched her skin. She did this several times, her tears mingling with the water, until she couldn't see straight.

"I need to tear my clothing," she mumbled, reaching for the collar of her shirt so that the fabric would rip over her heart, as was the Jewish custom for mourners. She grabbed the cotton with both hands and pulled in opposite directions. The fabric didn't tear.

I need to show I'm in mourning, she thought to herself. Rachel gripped another portion of the fabric, near the seam, and tugged as hard as she could. The cotton didn't budge. "I have to do this for Mother," she said, as she tried to tear the seam. "Why won't you tear?" she cried. "Why can't I do this?" She yanked the material one more time, ripping it apart. Then she collapsed, her head down and her arms splayed out in front of her.

上海

A small hand, Menahem's hand, began moving in circles on Rachel's back as the rabbi asked for the repose of her mother's soul. Menahem's tear-stained face made Rachel realize that in spite of his own sadness, he wanted to comfort her. She reached for Menahem and held him to her tightly. "Mother loved you as though you were her own son," she said through her tears when the rabbi had stopped talking. "You made her smile and laugh. You helped her feel better."

Nucia bent down, picked up a clump of earth with her hands, and threw it on their mother's coffin. Rachel did the same, followed by Menahem. The only other people at the funeral were Jacob, Shprintze, Isaac, baby Zelda, and Anna.

Everyone said the *kaddish*, the mourner's prayer invoking peace. As she recited the familiar words, Rachel considered the possibility of peace everywhere, then remembered Shprintze's brother, Anna's husband, and Yosef Trumpeldor, fighting for Russia, and the pogroms that continued in her country.

At the end of the kaddish, baby Zelda made a cooing sound.

Life goes on. We must go forward and live the lives we were meant to live, thought Rachel.

"We will be all right," she said aloud, wrapping her arms around Menahem. "It's going to be difficult, but we'll survive and get to America. I promise you."

Part Four

Summer/
Fall 1904

Mark this: As long as people are afraid, they will rot like birches in the marsh. We must grow bold; it is time!

—Maxim Gorky *[Russian novelist], Mother, 1907*

20

June 28, 1904
37 Foochow Road
Shanghai

Dear Sergei,

Mother died and we all miss her terribly. Menahem clings to me and Nucia as if he's afraid we're going to abandon him at any moment. I can't blame him for thinking this. In his short life he has lost so many people. It doesn't seem fair that one small child should have to bear so much pain.

Now, I'm more determined than ever to get to America. I feel as if we're cursed here in Shanghai, after Mother's death, and want to start over in a place far from here, far from the rain which comes down on us and never

*seems to end. Streets and rivers are flooded and the wet,
dank smell is unbearable. Menahem actually makes little
boats from twigs and paper and sails them in the puddles.*

*I read your letter in disbelief, unable to understand
why people who were found guilty of murder during the
Kishinev pogrom received such light punishments. No
matter how many times I read your words, I cannot make
sense of them. I've read about people who started strikes
receiving much longer and harsher punishments than the
murderers in Kishinev. Seeing the small value placed
on Jewish lives in Russia makes me glad to be out of the
country, and sad for those who cannot escape.*

I hope to hear from you again soon.
Your Rachel

*P.S. I love the drawings you've sent, and have hung them
in our hostel room so that they're the first things I see when
I wake up. Even with your injured hand, your talent is
obvious and is being wasted at the factory.*

"Rachel! What are you doing?" Nucia's voice interrupted
Rachel's writing.

"Writing a letter," she replied, holding her paper to her
chest so that Nucia couldn't see her words.

"It's the Sabbath. You know that writing is not allowed."
Nucia stood over Rachel like a tree blocking the sun. Menahem,
who had come in after Nucia, slunk into their cot.

"We broke many Sabbath customs traveling here, but you
never complained," said Rachel.

"That's different," Nucia retorted. "We had no choice."

"I have no choice now. I must write to Sergei." She paused and glanced down at her letter. "I need to write, to get my thoughts and fears on paper. It's as necessary to me as breathing."

"That's ridiculous." Nucia dropped heavily onto her cot. "Writing is not necessary for survival. You need to observe the Sabbath, to pray that our lives will be filled with divine blessings."

Rachel leaned toward Nucia. "I did observe the Sabbath in Kishinev, and look where it got us. Here, without Father and Mother, without a home, without hope. I'm tired of praying for things that never happen. Prayer isn't enough. We have to make choices and do things that will improve our lives, instead of hoping for divine help that will never come."

"You must not speak this way," said Nucia. "Not in front of Menahem."

"Father was killed because of his faith," said Rachel, standing and facing Nucia. "Mother died because of the long journey we were forced to take."

"But they never questioned their Judaism," argued Nucia.

"Maybe they should have."

"Rachel," asked Menahem in a small voice. "Can we be Jewish on the inside and not Jewish on the outside?"

Rachel strode to their cot and sat beside Menahem. "I'm not sure."

"I'm afraid to be Jewish. I'm scared to die."

Rachel held Menahem in her arms. "I won't let anything happen to you." She looked deeply into his teary face. "And you should always be proud of who you are. Though it's hard for me to have faith all the time, I'm still proud to be a Jew. One day, this hatred toward us will be gone and we'll be able to live anywhere we want without fear."

Menahem nodded and wrapped his arms around Rachel's waist. "So Yosef Trumpeldor won't have to worry about losing his other arm because the war will be over?" he asked her.

Rachel bit her lower lip and tried to think of the best words to say to Menahem. "I don't know that countries will ever stop fighting over land and water, but Jewish soldiers will be treated fairly."

"When will this happen?" Menahem let go of Rachel and looked up at her with expectant eyes.

"Not soon enough," she replied.

Menahem nodded, accepting her answer. He dragged the stool to the window so he could see the people walking outside.

Rachel lay down on her cot, her arms clasped behind her neck, her mind brewing with an idea.

上海

"I want to write about Jews fighting in the Russian-Japanese war," Rachel said, in a bold voice that surprised even herself.

Mr. Ezra lifted his head and gazed at her for a long time, without blinking. "So write it."

"I need help."

"So?" Mr. Ezra dropped his pen and folded his hands together. "You cannot do this on your own?"

"I need information, facts, and don't know where to find them."

Mr. Ezra cleared his throat, causing the skin around his neck to jiggle.

Rachel bit her bottom lip. "I want people to know how Jews are risking their lives for a country that despises us."

"It is a good story idea, but you must be able to separate your own feelings from the facts. I want the news, not your opinions."

"I understand," said Rachel.

Mr. Ezra stroked his whiskers and stood. "Somewhere in this mess I know I have…" He began rifling through stacks of newspapers. He mumbled to himself as he glanced at them, oblivious of Rachel.

Rachel watched closely, her eyebrows rising as he moved through the papers.

"Aha!" He picked up a number of papers and carried them back to his desk. "These are issues of a Russian newspaper that is being published to provide information about the Russian-Japanese War, the *Russkij Invalid* and…" Mr. Ezra flipped through an issue, page by page. "Here we are." He brought the issue over to Rachel.

She followed his finger to a list of Jewish names, men and boys who had been killed, injured, or were missing in action. "This is incredible, I had no idea this information existed," she said.

"Good sources are the most important tools for reporters," said Mr. Ezra. He shuffled back to his desk, gathered the rest of the issues of the *Russkij Invalid*, and dropped them into Rachel's arms. "This will give you a good start, just make sure you name the *Invalid* as your source in your story when you use their facts. You must always give credit where it's due."

"I will," said Rachel.

"And keep it short, to the point," added Mr. Ezra. He returned to his desk and sat down. "Three inches."

"Three inches?"

He scratched his head. "Two hundred and fifty words."

"All right." Rachel stood, her arms getting tired from holding the stack of newspapers.

"What are you still standing there for? Don't you have a story to write?"

"Yes." Rachel moved toward the door. "I promise it will be good, Mr. Ezra."

He grunted and waved her away.

上海

As soon as she returned to her room in the hostel, Rachel eagerly began going through the names in the *Russkij Invalid*, writing them down in her journal, along with information she considered important.

After two hours and hundreds of names, her hand ached from writing and she realized she had more information than she needed. She sat back on her cot and stared at the names she'd carefully recorded. *This isn't a story*, she thought with disdain. *This is a list*. She slammed her journal shut and tried to visualize the story in her head. But her mind grew too cluttered with names and dates.

Rachel took a deep breath and opened her journal to a crisp, white page and wrote, "Important Facts" across the top. She proceeded to list the points she wanted to make in her article, followed by the names she wanted to mention, and a brief summary of how the war affected Jews and Shanghai. She looked over what she'd written and the article began to evolve in her head. Afraid she'd lose her focus, Rachel bent over her journal and wrote until she had finished the piece.

21

RUSSIAN JEWS ARE FIGHTING A WAR FOR A
COUNTRY THAT DOESN'T WANT THEM

The Russian-Japanese War is having a profound impact
on Russian Jews who have either been drafted into service or volunteered. Though there have been reports of
Jews deserting to Germany, many others are demonstrat-
ing an incredible loyalty to their country, despite the fact
that Russia has been trying to get rid of its Jews for years.
Today, from notices that have appeared in the Russkij
Invalid newspaper since the war began, there are more
than two thousand Jewish soldiers taking part in the
Russian-Japanese War. Many of these men are either
injured or missing in action.

Yosef Trumpeldor, for example, left the safety of Shanghai to volunteer as a soldier for the Russian army in Port Arthur. A 24-year-old dentist, he has lost an arm during a battle at Port Arthur, but refuses to leave the front. He continues to fight for his country.

Dr. Henryk Goldszmit recently left Shanghai to work at a field hospital in Mukden, near Port Arthur. The interesting thing about Dr. Goldszmit is that he's not even Russian. He's from Poland and was one of the first Jews accepted to the Warsaw University to study medicine. Tevye Wilner had to leave his wife when he was drafted in Russia to join the army. Now his wife, Anna, is waiting anxiously for him to come back safely from his station in Port Arthur. Infrequent letters from Tevye are the only connection Anna has to her husband, and his words offer a rare insight to the life of a Jewish soldier. He has written about being segregated from Russian soldiers, not being able to join the artillery because he's Jewish, and being called a coward and a useless soldier by his commanders.

The Russian-Japanese War is for control of Port Arthur, an ice-free port in Manchuria that opens to the Yellow Sea. Since the Russian army greatly outnumbers the Japanese, this war was expected to last a short time. But the Japanese have proven to be formidable opponents and the war has become extensive, lengthy, and costly, with many land and sea battles.

The effects are being felt even here in Shanghai, which has been used as a blockade, a repair facility, a base of operation, and a refuge. This war has also led to the creation of the Red Cross Society of China on March 10, 1904, in Shanghai. The founders, Chinese business and political leaders, wanted to create a neutral group that would be able to enter Manchurian war zones to help civilians caught in the conflict.

Rachel read her article with a mixture of pride and annoyance. She stood in the *Israel's Messenger* office, holding one of the first copies of the weekly issue that had come off the press.

"Not bad," said Mr. Ezra. He stood across from her at a tall table, the newspaper spread out in front of him as well.

"I just wish my name could be there," sighed Rachel.

"You know that's not possible, not now anyway," said Mr. Ezra.

"Yes, but I won't be happy until my name can be printed with my story."

"You're certainly persistent," smiled Mr. Ezra. "I imagine your father would be proud of you right now."

Rachel bit her bottom lip and nodded.

Mr. Ezra opened the pouch around his waist and pulled out some coins. "Here you are." He reached across the table and dropped the coins in front of Rachel, eight jiao.

"This much, for one story?" She gasped and touched the coins lightly.

"Don't get a big head now," warned Mr. Ezra. "You took twice as long as you should have to write the story, and I still had to edit it."

Rachel carefully picked up the coins and held them tightly in her hand. "Next time, I promise I'll be quicker and better."

"All right, all right." Mr. Ezra folded the newspaper and shoved it aside. "Now go, I've got a lot of work to do here."

Rachel marched to the door, her head held high. "I'll be back with another story idea soon."

"You do that," said Mr. Ezra, without looking up from his desk.

上海

Since her mother's death, Rachel had trouble sleeping. She woke early every day and paced the streets of Shanghai taking in everything that she saw around her. This morning, Rachel walked south along the banks of the Huangpu River and headed toward Nanking Road. She turned right and marched briskly through the central business district. Rickshaw drivers, in triangular straw hats, gathered, waiting for their first fares of the day. Beggars looked at her with pleading gazes, opium addicts with dilated eyes staggered precariously, and families sat listlessly outside the shelter for indigent newcomers. A pack of Jews crowded the doorway of this shelter now, women with babies, elderly men broken with age, children with defeat in their faces.

Rachel quickened her pace to get past the shelter, slowing only when she came to the French Concession. Here, the streets widened and extravagant homes and shops lined the boulevard. A private rickshaw moved past Rachel, carrying a wealthy Baghdad Jew dressed in a turban and a long flowing robe that flapped against the rickshaw as he went by. These Jews had organized successful businesses in Shanghai and had a major influence here and in other countries. Though they shared the same faith, they were as foreign to her as the Chinese people.

From what she'd read in the *Israel's Messenger*, Rachel knew the Baghdad Jews already had wealth when they arrived in Shanghai, unlike the destitute Jews who came as refugees from Russia. *How can we ever make enough money to be successful if we continue to be stuck in low-paying jobs?* she thought. Perhaps this could be the subject of her next article for Mr. Ezra.

In her head, Rachel began making a list of what she needed to do for this story—interview Russian refugees, Baghdad Jews, and employers. Ideas and plans flooded her mind as she continued walking briskly to her job at the laundry.

22

Sergei sat with Pavel and a few other men at a dimly lit tavern near the factory. He stared at a man sitting at a nearby table. He recognized this man, but couldn't place him.

The mysterious man tapped his glass against his comrade's, then turned toward Sergei, revealing a nervous twitch in his nose. Just then, Sergei realized who he was—Boris Savinkov, head of the Combat Organization, a secret group that was notorious for assassinating government officials. Its goal was to force the government into making political compromises in favor of the workers. Sergei recognized his face from a recent photo in the party's newspaper, *Revolutionary Russia*.

"That's Boris Savinkov," whispered Sergei to Pavel.

"Boris who?" said Pavel, his voice rising.

"Don't talk so loudly. He's been in exile for killing the Minister of the Interior years ago."

"What's he doing here?"

"Maybe he escaped and is looking for men to join the Combat Organization."

Pavel eyed Sergei with suspicion. "You'd have to have a death wish to get involved with that organization."

"Yes," said Sergei. "You would."

When Savinkov departed, Sergei left the tavern without a word to Pavel, who was busy drinking and laughing with the other men at their table. Their voices blurred to a dim murmur as Sergei opened the door and stepped outside. A harsh wind swatted his face, but Sergei kept moving with long strides to catch up to the man in front of him.

"Please sir," said Sergei in a breathless voice, as he caught up to the slender man bundled in a sheepskin coat. "May I have a word with you?"

Savinkov glanced sideways at Sergei but did not slow his pace. "Who are you?"

"Sergei Khanzhenkov. I work at the Putilov factory."

"What can I do for you, Khanzhenkov?"

"I've read about you and your radical group and I like the bold actions you take to get what you want."

"Where are you from, Khanzhenkov?"

"Kishinev. I lived there during the massacre and saw how the police, under Viacheslav von Plehve's orders, did nothing to protect the Jews. I saw the police laughing and talking as Jews were tortured. People like von Plehve should be punished for the murders he allowed, but the government has done nothing. Instead he remains in power as Interior Minister of Police."

Savinkov stopped and turned sharply so that he faced Sergei. "And just what do you think should happen to von Plehve?"

"He should be sentenced to exile."

"Too good for a devil such as von Plehve!" scoffed Savinkov.

"You think he should be killed?"

"What I think and what will happen are two very different matters. I have no say in his fate. I know nothing of this radical group you speak of."

A light rain began to fall; drops landed on Sergei's nose, leaving his skin wet and cold. "But I read about you and the Combat Organization in the newspaper. It's the group that Grigorii Gershuni founded…"

"Gershuni has just been sentenced to a life term of hard labor." Savinkov held up a gloved hand. "Do you really think I would risk my freedom again, after escaping from two years of exile in Vologda?" He clenched his collar tightly around his neck and resumed walking.

Sergei watched the evasive man disappear into the haze of streetlights. The damp air wet his clothes and his skin as he headed to the factory barracks. After discarding his soggy clothing, he crawled into his bunk and pulled the threadbare, itchy blanket over his head.

上海

The Petersburg church reminded Sergei of Sunday mornings in Kishinev, tightly packed with people, hardly any room to breathe. There was the mandatory eastern wall of icons with their pious scenes, and the sweet-scented incense that didn't quell the inevitable body odor. Even the chanting sounded the same, as if the people from his hometown had been uprooted and moved to this church. Except here there were an unusually high number of factory workers, because of the mandatory church attendance demanded by the Putilov factory.

His eyes slid around the cathedral, taking in the people whose lips moved in unison, reciting Bible passages from memory. Here, in church, factory workers like him stood together with rich business owners and apprentices. A false sense of equality infused these walls. *When the service ends*, thought Sergei to himself, *we will no longer be equals.* Sergei clamped his mouth shut and stared blankly at the priest.

A powerful thud landed across Sergei's lower back as he moved with the crowd from the church when the service had finished. He jerked his head around to see who had hit him and found himself eye-to-eye with a grave-faced man in his early twenties. The man blinked and shoved a piece of paper into Sergei's right hand. Sergei looked down at his hand, then up again, only to find that the man had vanished. Sergei scoured the area for a glimpse of the stranger, but did not see him anywhere. It seemed as if he had been an illusion, except for the very tangible piece of paper in his sweaty palm.

As soon as he could break free from the swarm surrounding the church, Sergei bolted toward the trolley headed for the center of Petersburg where he could examine the paper in his hand without worrying about being seen.

143 Rizhsky prospekt 8:00 tonight.

Sergei scratched his head and read the brief message three times as he sat in the half-empty trolley. He pictured the man who had given him this note and tried to recall if he'd ever seen him before. No, never.

After getting off the trolley near the Winter Palace, Sergei stuffed the note in his pocket and strolled along the Dvortsovaya nab, which hugged the bank of the Neva River. He shaded his face with his hand and gazed out at the turquoise water. It looked cool and inviting with the hot afternoon sun shining down on it.

Sergei resumed walking past the Peter and Paul Fortress, built by Peter the Great almost two hundred years earlier. Usually, he stopped to admire the stone building with its gilded, angel-topped cupola and its bell tower that soared higher than any other structure in Petersburg. But the mysterious note distracted him and filled his imagination with all kinds of possibilities. He drew in a long breath and kept walking, his fists curled into balls, his shoulders hunched forward.

Rizhsky Prospekt, a long, narrow street, ran east of the Neva River, about halfway between the Ekspedisia factory and the center of Petersburg. Under the dim oil street lamps, Sergei peered at the numbers until he came to a nondescript two-storey building wedged tightly between a tavern and a smoke shop. He looked left and right before tapping the door tentatively.

The door opened slightly.

"Your name?" said an unfamiliar rumbling voice.

"Sergei Khanzhenkov."

Silence. The door opened wider. Sergei stepped inside to a cold, damp room with an unlit stove to the left, and a round table surrounded by seven people. Sergei hesitated when he saw the first man seated to his right—Boris Savinkov. This was a secret meeting with Boris Savinkov. The man who'd opened the door took a seat beside a petite young woman with dark, round eyes and gestured for Sergei to sit in the one remaining chair next to Savinkov.

Sergei's stomach lurched uncomfortably as he sat down. It had been two weeks since he'd spoken to Savinkov, two weeks since Savinkov had denied any involvement with this group. Now, in this secluded room, surrounded by strangers, Sergei began to regret his impulsive behavior.

"Does anybody know why we're all here?" began Savinkov, looking at the faces around the table. "I certainly have no idea."

Sergei creased his brow and looked around the room. One middle-aged man with spectacles grinned, as if he'd heard something funny. The one woman in the room did not look amused.

"I can think of a hundred other ways to spend my time, rather than sitting here playing guessing games with a bunch of slow-wits," said Savinkov. "Khanzhenkov, do you know why you're here?"

Sergei's face grew red and warm. "To talk about the Combat Organization?"

"To talk about the Combat Organization?" Savinkov rubbed his chin with his thumb and forefinger. "And then after we talk about it, we will simply leave?"

Sergei slouched in his chair.

"In case the rest of you are of the same pathetic mind as Khanzhenkov, let me explain." Savinkov paused and lit a cigarette. "This is the Combat Organization and, unlike the Revolutionary Party, we spend more time doing and less time talking. Only through actions can we be successful in our quest to bring power to the people. There are many people in Russia who would like to see us vanish altogether. But this is impossible, for we are as necessary as wood for a fire." He folded his well-scrubbed hands and looked shrewdly around the table. "Nothing we speak of tonight can be repeated outside to others. Is that understood?" He scrunched his cigarette in the bottom of an empty glass.

Sergei, along with every person around the table, nodded solemnly.

"This group does not exist outside these walls," Savinkov continued.

"What are we planning, Boris?" asked the man with round spectacles, directly across from Sergei.

"All in good time, Egor," replied Savinkov. "All in good time." He lit another cigarette and inhaled before continuing. "My predecessor, Grigorii Gershuni, did a fair job as leader of this combat organization and had good intentions. But, alas, he failed and has been caught because he acted hastily, without a well thought-out plan." His eyes roamed around the table, stopping at every person for a second. "We will not make the same mistakes. We will plan meticulously and we will be successful."

Sergei thought about Gershuni, now exiled to hard labor, and shuddered.

"The first thing we must do is create a better weapon for our purpose," said Savinkov. He rose and began pacing as he spoke in a voice that radiated with conviction. "Guns are not as effective as we need them to be. We're going to use bombs, which is why Max and Dora are here." He nodded at the oldest person in the room, a white-haired man, and the woman, fragile yet beautiful with pale skin and long brown hair in a loose braid. "Max is an expert in chemical engineering and Dora brings to us her vast knowledge of explosives."

Sergei couldn't stop from staring at the petite woman who looked barely strong enough to clean a house, let alone make bombs.

"Now," continued Savinkov, twirling his whiskers with his fingers. He stopped pacing and wrapped his hands over the back of his chair. "Before we go any further, I need to make sure all of you are fully committed to this organization." He looked directly at Sergei. "If you have any doubts, any fears, any criticism, leave now. There is room for only one leader in this group and there is no place for weaklings."

Sergei swallowed and flinched under Savinkov's penetrating gaze. From the corner of his eye, he saw Boris sit upright, with an almost bored expression on his pasty face. Dora sat perfectly serene, as if she was where she wanted to be, doing exactly what she wanted to do. Sergei glanced at the door and, for a second, considered jumping up and dashing outside. The price he might have to pay would be steep. It could even be his life.

Then Sergei looked down at his mangled hand and thought about the uncertainty he felt every day, not knowing if he'd keep his job because of his decreased productivity. He remembered others unable to work at all because of on-the-job injuries. He thought about Lev, missing, either exiled or dead, and how much Lev had wanted things to get better for factory workers.

Sergei sat up taller in his seat and set his mouth in a hard line. His stomach knotted up as he returned Savinkov's unwavering gaze. Sergei knew that now there would be no turning back. He would become a member of the Combat Organization with all of its risks and consequences.

Even Papa would be impressed.

23

"Your biggest advantage is your age," said Savinkov, without taking his eyes from the horses racing around the dusty track.

The white night sun glowed like a star, setting the sky on fire. Violet clouds hung low over the horses, cantering like graceful performers on a stage. "Nobody will suspect a sixteen-year-old of being anything but a newsboy," Savinkov continued.

At this moment, Sergei finally understood that he had been recruited to be part of the Combat group because of his age. "Who is our target? Von Plehve?"

Savinkov jumped to his feet, screaming at the horses rounding the last corner of the track. A mixture of cheers and boos rang from the crowd when the horses passed the finish line. A glistening black horse with a patch of white on his neck came first, followed closely by a reddish-brown horse.

"Dammit!" said Savinkov. He crumpled the piece of paper

he held in his hand and sat down, his face flushed and sweaty. He sighed heavily. "You'll find out the target when I'm ready to tell you. The less you know right now, the better. Just watch the comings and goings of government members and learn all their routines and their habits."

Sergei opened his mouth to speak, but Savinkov abruptly turned to talk to someone else. Without another word to Sergei, Savinkov rose and sauntered away. Sergei remained sitting, his gaze on Savinkov's authoritative figure until he disappeared into the boisterous crowd. With his lips set in a hard line, Sergei stood and joined the horde of people moving slowly toward the entrance of the track. His stomach tightened uncomfortably as he walked out of the track. Nerves. Anticipation. Fear.

A tavern stood conveniently right outside the gates of the horse track. Sergei paused outside the door and listened to the men's voices, animated by generous amounts of alcohol. He thought longingly of sleep in the barracks, but remembered how he'd tossed and turned lately, how sleep had been as elusive as good luck or happiness. A couple of drinks might help loosen his stomach, calm his anxiety, let him to sleep for a few hours.

Straightening his shoulders, Sergei opened the door and stepped into the smoky, lively tavern where he remained until the first rays of morning sun appeared through the small window. Later he staggered back to the barracks, his head heavy as an iron pot. He collapsed on his cot into a fitful slumber.

上海

It had been several weeks since Sergei had switched to the night shift at the factory so that he could pretend to be a newsboy during the day. This morning, he would be starting at a new location, on the Izmailovskii Prospekt, a street that led to the train station. The mid-July sun warmed his face and hands, and the surge of people moving in every direction kept him from getting bored. Other vendors stood nearby, selling oranges, tea, nuts, and blini.

"Newspapers! Get your newspaper!" Sergei shouted out to a large group of well-dressed people walking through an archway out of the station. The pleasant scent of mignonette and oleander wafted into Sergei's nose as the group drew closer to him. One woman, holding a parasol above her unnaturally pale face, smiled at Sergei with saccharine lips.

"I'll take one," said one of the men in the group, wearing a frock coat and duck trousers. He handed Sergei the money and took a paper.

Sergei gave the man a closed-lip smile and observed his companions to determine if any were government workers. Satisfied that they were simply ordinary Russians, Sergei turned his attention to a government carriage that approached the station. It was an open carriage that offered a good look at its occupant. Sergei froze when he spotted Interior Minister Viacheslav von Plehve—the man who had allowed the Kishinev pogrom that had killed Rachel's father and so many others.

At once, Sergei recognized the double chin, the bushy white whiskers above his upper lip, the round face. Sergei checked the time on the watch Savinkov had given him. Five minutes after ten. If von Plehve traveled this route every day, then he would be easy prey. Savinkov hadn't yet told any of the members of the Combat Organization the name of their target, but Sergei knew it would be von Plehve. He could feel it in his veins when he talked to Savinkov, from the way Sakinov's tone sharpened when the Interior Minister's name crossed his lips.

Sergei's stomach knotted up when his eyes met von Plehve's as the carriage drove past. In that brief second, Sergei saw a darkness in von Plehve's piercing gaze that chilled him right to the bone.

上海

They gathered in an abandoned shop ten blocks from Sergei's barracks. Meetings had been held in different locations to avoid a routine that might be recognized by the police. This time all eighteen members of the Combat Organization were present, and an undercurrent of anticipation filled the smoky air. Sergei, sat around the table amongst the others, tapping the floor impatiently. Sweat trickled from under his arms and the back of his neck.

"Welcome, comrades," said Savinkov. Conversations immediately receded to silence. "We have been watching and waiting quietly and patiently. It will soon be time to act." He paused and surveyed the room with a penetrating gaze.

"Our target is von Plehve."

Sergei exhaled and listened as Sakinov explained why von Plehve had to be executed.

"Twenty years ago, von Plehve put innocent people into the stone dungeons of the fortresses of Peter and Paul. He ordered harsh persecutions, contrary to the laws of the Muscovite Empire. People died by the dozens. Von Plehve has continued to support murderous attacks on intellectuals, workmen, Jews, and peasants in Russia, most recently, the Kishinev and Gomel pogroms. Yet he retains his respected position within the government. It is time to get rid of him.

"We will surprise von Plehve during his morning journey to the Tsar's residence in Peterhof," explained Sakinov. "We're going to use dynamite to create a bomb. Dora will take care of this."

Sergei jerked his head in Dora's direction. Her enormous eyes blinked calmly, as if she'd been asked to make tea.

"Would you explain why dynamite is the best choice?" Savinkov asked Dora.

All eyes fell on the only female present, the only female in this secret organization.

She folded her dainty hands and rested her forearms on the table. "Though dynamite costs more than gunpowder and revolvers," she began, in a quiet, steady voice, "and is more likely to kill innocent people near the target, it is without question, most effective. In fact, the explosive force of nitroglycerine compared with gunpowder is thirteen to one."

Dora continued speaking, but Sergei found himself thinking about the crowd surrounding von Plehve as he drove past him each day—his driver, the horses, and all the innocent people walking on the street nearby. Nausea rose from the pit of his stomach; he stifled the urge to vomit and forced himself to pay attention.

Dora spoke bluntly about the hazards of dynamite, how it was dangerous to transport and how explosions could occur during the formation. Hearing about explosions made everything seem so real, he thought, too absolute and too permanent. Until now, he'd been conducting harmless surveillance. He wanted von Plehve dead, or at least he'd thought he did, but now he couldn't be sure of what he wanted. The man's death would not replace the lives he'd taken. Nor would it return Kishinev back to the comfortable town it had been for him before the riots.

Sergei turned his head and looked at the door, directly across from Savinkov. He considered the possibility of crouching down and crawling out of the room and realized how futile this would be, how he would immediately be seen and caught, how Savinkov had already murdered at least two people, and was planning another attack.

There is no way out. Maybe Papa was right. Maybe I am a coward.

上海

Sergei, dressed in a railway worker's uniform, with oversized spectacles and a cap pulled low over his brow, walked a couple of steps behind Egor and Max, who had also been assigned to this mission. It was a clear July morning, without a cloud in the sky, yet Sergei's feet felt as heavy as iron. He stared straight ahead along Izmailovskii Prospekt in an attempt to ignore the twelve-pound bomb concealed as an ordinary package.

"You will be the decoy," Savinkov had explained to Sergei two nights earlier. "Egor will throw the bomb. Then you and Max will push people around so that nobody sees who did this. All they will remember are railway workers, and there are hundreds of these in Petersburg."

Now, every muscle in Sergei's body tensed when he heard the clip-clop of horse's feet along the pavement. As the horses carrying von Plehve's carriage drew closer, on schedule, doom settled uncomfortably on Sergei's shoulders. The carriage appeared on his left, moving at a brisk pace, the horses trotting majestically along the street. Policemen stood at attention as the carriage rolled past. Horse-drawn cabs moved over to the side of the road to let the government official go by.

Just as von Plehve's carriage approached the bridge over the Obvodnyi Canal, Egor stepped forward. As soon as the carriage came directly beside Egor, he threw his bomb at Plehve, setting off an instant explosion that erupted into the blue sky. Egor, who was supposed to run away, had been knocked off his feet by an officer's bicycle. Sergei froze and stared at the flames and smoke. His face started to get hot. From the corner of his eye, he saw Max run off in the direction of the Neva River. Egor lay still on the street, surrounded by police officers.

Sergei backed away from the pile of wood that used to be a carriage, from the horses, blown off their feet, lying on their sides, mounds of innocent dead flesh. Agonizing screams and smoke lingered in the chaotic air as he stepped backwards. A man lay groaning on the street, his trousers torn and bloody from his knees down to his feet. Several women and men were sprawled on the ground, their faces covered in blood and ash from the explosion.

"What the devil happened?" a woman cried out.

"Get the doctor," someone else yelled.

Sergei spun around and saw a swarthy man staring at him warily, his forehead creased with thick lines. Sergei jerked his head away from the man and began running. He didn't stop until he arrived safely behind the door of the barracks, out of breath. The screams of horror echoed in his head, along with the shattering sound of the bombs destroying everything in their path.

He paced back and forth, reminding himself that he had wanted this to happen. This was the revenge he sought for Rachel and the other Jews who had suffered in the Kishinev pogrom. Instead, he felt hollow inside, as though he were grieving the loss of someone he knew. Himself. Now he seemed no better than the people who had killed Jews in Kishinev. No better than his father who had stood by and watched as innocent people were killed.

24

Rachel dumped a pile of dirty linen into the tub of hot water, but her mind was not on her work. She was preoccupied by her article, fixated on the trouble she'd faced in getting an employer to speak to her for her article about getting ahead in Shanghai. Rachel had approached a dozen business owners but not one had agreed to speak to her because she was a girl. Even though she had some good interviews with other working Jews, she was not even close to having a finished story.

"What is wrong with you?"

The manager's sharp voice cut through the thick, damp air like a knife. Rachel yanked the linen she'd been washing from the tub, drenching her legs and feet.

"You've been staring at the wall for fifteen minutes without moving," the manager continued. He moved closer so that his face was inches from Rachel's. "Have you forgotten what you're here to do?"

"No," said Rachel.

"Just to make sure, you'll stay an hour late today."

Anna gave Rachel a sympathetic look. Rachel dumped her linen back in the water and scrubbed until her hands grew numb and raw. As she worked, she recalled the chiding voices of the men who had rejected her request for an interview: "Go back home, where you belong." "You should be cooking, not writing…"

An hour after everyone else had gone home, Rachel stepped out of the laundry and found Nucia waiting for her in the lavender twilight.

"What are you doing here? Where's Menahem?" asked Rachel wearily. She rubbed her aching shoulder with her hand.

"He's at the hostel with Jacob. I wanted to talk to you."

"Oh?"

They began walking down the narrow, winding road toward the corner. A soft glow from the oil lamps overhead lit the street.

"Jacob has asked me to marry him," said Nucia, the words spilling out of her mouth.

Rachel twirled her braid with her finger and kept her eyes on the ground. "What did you say?"

Nucia faced Rachel and reached for her hands. "Rachel, I said yes."

"I'm happy for you," said Rachel.

Nucia, her eyes shining, released Rachel's hands and resumed walking. "I never expected to find someone for myself. I thought a groom would be chosen by Mother and Father."

"It's better this way."

"Do you think Mother and Father would approve of Jacob?" asked Nucia.

"I'm sure they would." Rachel slowed her pace. "And they'd be very happy to see our family grow."

Nucia flung her arms around her sister. They stood, clinging to one another, their faces streaked with tears.

"That's not all," Nucia continued, after they'd started walking again.

"What do you mean?"

"Jacob doesn't want to stay in Shanghai. He wants to go to America."

"He does?"

"Yes, and he's saved enough for my passage and his, which means you can have what I've earned for yourself and Menahem. We can finally apply for our papers to go to America together!"

Rachel grabbed her sister's shoulders and pulled her into the tightest embrace she could manage after fourteen hours of washing clothes. "When is the wedding?"

上海

"How will Sergei find us, all the way in America?" asked Menahem. He, Rachel, and Nucia sat by the river, dangling their feet in the cool water. Jacob couldn't be there as he and Nucia were getting married in five days and, according to Jewish tradition, the bride and groom weren't allowed to see each other for one week before the big day.

Children's laughter rang out in the thick, humid late September air. The trees' leaves sagged and wilted.

"When we arrive in America, I'll send him a letter telling him where we're living," said Rachel.

"How far is America?" asked Menahem.

"Farther than we've come from Kishinev," Rachel began. "About six thousand miles, on the other side of the ocean."

Menahem said nothing; he just stared at the water.

Rachel jumped up and took Menahem's hand. "I'm so hot I'm afraid I'll melt if I don't get in the water." She pulled him up and they ran into the river.

"Are there rivers in America?" asked Menahem when his head popped through the surface.

"Yes, lots of rivers, lots of everything—jobs, schools, and food." Rachel splashed Menahem's face. "Best of all, we will be safe there."

Menahem moved his arms up and down through the water, splashing Rachel in the face. Rachel stuck her head under the water and grabbed his legs. She threw him up so that he came flying out of the water and fell back in, head first.

A moment later, she felt a hand on her shin. Menahem tried to knock her off her feet. She pretended to lose her balance and went under. The instant quiet and solitude beneath the water enveloped Rachel, gave her a sense of peace that seemed impossible to feel above water. It was as if time stopped as she floated, weightless. She stayed under as long as she could, until her lungs craved oxygen. Then she soared to the surface and took a big gulp of air.

上海

The wedding took place by Suzhou Creek, under a crown of trees that served as the *chupah*, the canopy which symbolized the roof of Jacob and Nucia's new home. Ironic, thought Rachel, considering that they had no actual home and would be leaving Shanghai as soon as their papers arrived.

A glorious day dawned for the wedding, with an endless blue sky. Nucia wore a simple white dress made by some of her seamstress friends that fit snugly around her bosom and waist and fell gracefully to the ground. On her head, a white scarf concealed everything except her eyes. Jacob had borrowed black trousers and a white shirt with sleeves that were too short.

Rachel nudged Nucia and they marched toward the chupah. Upon reaching Jacob, Rachel escorted Nucia around him seven times to symbolize their union.

As she guided Nucia around the seventh time, Rachel heard Zelda cry out as if she, a baby, recognized the significance of this Jewish custom. Rachel glanced over at Zelda, swaddled in Shprintze's arms, and smiled. Shprintze, Isaac, Anna, Yiehl Mendelssohn, and Danka Muller sat on the grassy hill overlooking the ceremony.

The rabbi said a blessing and drank from a cup of wine. He handed the cup to Jacob, who took a sip and then handed it to Nucia who did the same.

"You are hereby sanctified to me with this ring according to the Laws of Moses and Israel," said Jacob, placing a simple gold ring he'd purchased from a Chinese stall on Nucia's slender finger.

Rachel looked at Jacob and for the first time, realized that with this marriage, she had gained a brother. This thought made her more content than she'd been in a long time.

She thought about Sergei and wondered if marriages between Jews and Gentiles took place in America. Did love matter more than faith? Jacob grinned and smashed a glass with his right foot, bringing the ceremony to an end. This Jewish ritual was meant to remind people that even on happy occasions, they should remember the destruction of the Temple. Jacob enfolded Nucia in his arms, then broke away and hoisted a beaming Menahem onto his shoulders.

"I'm so happy for you," Rachel said to Nucia. "Mother and Father would be so proud."

Nucia's eyes shone with elation and tears. She took Rachel's hands and clasped them firmly in hers. "Today is the beginning of a new life for all of us," Nucia said. "Good things lie ahead for us. I can feel this as strongly as I feel my heart beating."

Rachel's lips quivered as she let herself be swept up in Nucia's embrace. Maybe Nucia would be right. Maybe now, Rachel hoped, they could put their difficult past behind and embrace the future.

25

July 17, 1904
Barracks No. 6
Putilov Factory
47, Stachek Avenue
Petersburg, Russia

Dear Rachel,

I am sorry for not writing sooner. Many times I have started a letter, only to rip it up because I have nothing new to say. Now, much has happened. Interior Minister von Plehve was killed two days ago. When I first heard this news, I felt relieved and gratified to know that he had paid the ultimate price for his despicable actions against the Kishinev Jews.

But my sense that Plehve's murder was justified

*became quickly overshadowed by confusion. His death
will not bring your father back. His death will not make
it safer for you in Russia. His death will not change
Russia. Yet people support the radical group that arranged
his assassination. There is almost a celebratory atmosphere
in the streets, as if Lent has just ended. Except a man has
been killed. His life was taken as a punishment, "an eye
for an eye." But nothing is better because he is gone. His
murder was as senseless as the ones in Kishinev, starting with our old friend Mikhail who was killed by his
relatives.*

*I've been thinking about Mikhail a lot lately. He
and I had planned to come to Petersburg together, to go
to university. Instead, he's dead and I have veered so far
from my dreams, I feel like a different person. A useless
person wasting my life away. I need to change. I need to
do something to improve my circumstances, to become a
better person.*

*Hopefully, the next time you hear from me, I will
have good news. I want to be proud of myself. But more
important, I want you and Menahem to be proud of me.*

Your Sergei

Sergei moved slowly through the crowded sidewalk. It had
been one week since the bombing, and he was on his way to
meet Sakinov in the Summer Garden.

"If you ask me, those rebels deserve medals for getting rid
of von Plehve," he heard a shopkeeper say loudly to a group of
men in front of his shop.

Sergei stopped walking and listened.

"I don't have any medals to give them," an older gentleman replied. "But you can be sure I'll be sending some money their way."

"So will I," said another man. "I'd like to see them take out all the corrupt government officials. Maybe then we can start with a clean slate."

Laughter burst from the mouths of every man in the group.

Sergei tugged each of his earlobes and continued down the street.

"It's hard not to feel happy about Plehve being killed."

Sergei jerked his head to the right and saw two middle-aged women absorbed in conversation. "The way my husband is dancing around with joy, you'd think *he'd* thrown the bomb at the minister," said the older of the two, whose cheeks puffed out when she smiled.

The women's laughter rang in Sergei's ears, fading when he came upon the Summer Garden, where the Fontanka River flowed out of the Neva River. With almost thirty minutes until he had to meet Savinkov, he joined the parade of strollers on the wide avenue through the garden, admiring the vibrant pink blossoms laid out in a geometric sequence of patterned flower beds. Lavender scented the air taking him back, if only for a moment, to Kishinev where lilacs bloomed all summer.

Sergei paused when he got to one of the fountains in the garden that represented Aesop's Fables. The Fountain depicted the story of "The Wind and the Sun," with a figure of the wind blowing hard on the man who formed the base of the fountain. The sun, much larger and higher than the wind, embodied the quiet, gentle strength that eventually led to the man throwing his cape on the ground. Though the wind looked strong, it was not enough to get the man to remove his cape. The sun and its gentleness had been able to do what force could not. As he gazed at the fountain, Sergei suddenly realized what he had to say to Savinkov.

上海

"Egor has woken from his coma," said Savinkov in a grave tone. He and Sergei sat down on a bench in the Summer Garden, near the Palace embankment.

"That's a relief," said Sergei, watching a group of children running past. The right side of his mouth twitched upwards. The pleasant smell of cologne, wafting from Savinkov's face, made Sergei turn back to his comrade.

"Or perhaps he may wish he were back in a coma." Savinkov lit his cigarette. "He's already been indicted for murder." He sucked on his cigarette and exhaled. "If only that damn officer hadn't been there."

"I'm not going to do this anymore," Sergei blurted out.

Savinkov straightened his silk cravat and gave him a long, hard look.

"This isn't me," Sergei continued, stumbling over his words. "I never meant to kill anybody."

"You didn't kill Plehve. Egor did."

"But I watched Plehve for weeks. I'm the one who told you about his schedule. I'm just as responsible as Egor."

Savinkov crossed his leg and puffed thoughtfully on his cigarette. "Nobody's stopping you from turning yourself in."

"I don't want to be part of your organization anymore," said Sergei.

"Are you crazy?"

"Maybe, a little. But at least I'll be able to sleep at night."

Savinkov dropped his cigarette in the dirt and crushed it with his foot. "I can't just let you walk away. How do I know I can trust you, that you won't turn in the members of the Combat Organization?"

Sergei swallowed before answering naively. "I guess you'll have to take my word."

"That's not enough."

"What do you mean?" Sergei held his breath and stared at Savinkov.

As Savinkov rose, his shadow loomed over Sergei. "You knew what we were going to do that night you asked if you could be part of this organization. You wanted Plehve dead as much as anyone else. It's too late for remorse. You're in too deep." He clasped his hands behind his back and sauntered away as casually as if he'd just invited Sergei to the opera.

Sergei's bottom lip dropped open. Savinkov disappeared into the crowd. Suddenly, Sergei realized he could never leave the Combat Organization—unless he left Russia altogether. He hunched forward, rested his elbows on his knees, and stared blankly at the people walking past.

I need money to get out of Russia, more money than I'll ever make in the factory. Sergei frowned at his injured hand for a moment, then sat upright. Determination narrowed his eyes. As the sun began to set over the trees in the garden, Sergei strode briskly to the trolley that would take him back to the barracks and to Pavel.

上海

"Together we are strong," read the caption on the top of the poster. It depicted a group of workers, arm in arm, standing in front of a factory. Doubt crossed Sergei's face as he squinted at the disproportionate workers' bodies. Their arms were twice as large as they should have been, emphasizing the idea of unity. The simplicity of the lines, the lack of details, the obvious exaggeration made Sergei cringe.

This poster, his first for the Revolutionary Party's recruitment campaign, was the beginning of his occupation as a propaganda artist—and perhaps the end of his dream to become an architect. As an architect, he'd be willing and proud to write his name beside his work. As a propaganda artist, he had to sign a false name to his drawing—Belov—to keep the police from discovering his identity. He had to work in a secret place and could tell nobody what he did. Except for Pavel, who'd helped him get this work. He couldn't even write to Rachel about this new turn of events in his life, since he was afraid his letters might be intercepted by the authorities.

But the money he made, ten times more than he received working in the factory, meant he could send more to his mother and sister. And just maybe he could save enough money for a journey to America—and a new life. With a heavy sigh, Sergei dipped his pen into the ink and continued to work on his poster.

26

"Come with me."

Sergei looked up from the letter he was writing to his mother when he heard Pavel's insistent voice.

"Where?" asked Sergei.

"I'll tell you on the way to the tavern."

Sergei glanced at his letter to his mother which he'd been struggling with for an hour. He'd only written two sentences. He dropped it on his cot and followed Pavel out of the barracks.

"Have you heard of Father George Gapon?" Pavel asked as soon as they were outside.

"A priest?"

Pavel steered Sergei to the left, toward the trolley stop, as they left the factory grounds. "Not just any priest, he's a big supporter of workers' rights."

"How can a priest help workers?"

"He's been a popular working class leader for years, and he organizes peaceful meetings."

The trolley arrived. They climbed on, dropped their kopecks into the fare container, and took seats at the back.

"The police don't bother him," Pavel continued. "I've heard that some policemen even attend Gapon's meetings."

"Really?" said Sergei.

"We'll see in a few minutes. He'll be speaking at the tearoom."

Sergei grunted and stared out the window at the trees, bare and gray, ready for winter.

The Petersburg Tearoom was hazy with smoke and humming with the steady sound of voices. The room was full. Sergei and Pavel had to crowd into the back. Pavel gestured to the server for two vodkas. When his drink arrived, Sergei emptied the vodka into his mouth as if it were water and looked furtively around the room for police. He didn't want to be here, where he was easy prey for Cossacks and the police. But alcohol numbed his fears and eased his throbbing head.

"Another?" asked Pavel, setting his glass down on a round table littered with empty glasses.

Sergei nodded. Pavel ordered two more, and began talking to a group of men behind him. Sergei recognized a few people from his factory. But most were strangers, workers from other factories. A few were missing fingers and one man with white hair and whiskers had a stump where his foot should have been. Sergei knew these men had been injured while working. He looked down at his own scarred hand.

"This your first meeting?"

An elbow jutted into Sergei's waist, almost knocking him over. He scowled and looked to his right where an impossibly thin boy stood grinning as if he were at a festival. Sergei nodded curtly and turned away.

"I've heard Gapon a few times," said the boy in a baritone voice that sounded strange, coming from such a young-looking face, with freckles sprinkled across his nose and cheeks. "Where're you working?"

Sergei didn't want to be noticed. He glanced to his left to see if he could move away from the boy, but didn't see an inch to spare. Men stood pressed against one another, much like Sunday services at the cathedral. "Putilov factory," answered Sergei reluctantly.

"I worked at the Semyannikov factory as an apprentice, until I was dismissed for helping organize a strike two years ago."

"You were dismissed?" Sergei peered at the boy more closely.

The boy nodded. "And blacklisted. I haven't had steady work since. Nobody will hire a striker. I've been working in a few small workshops, but the pay's so bad it doesn't even cover rent."

Sergei tried to imagine this innocent-looking boy organizing workers, being a leader, but couldn't. "How old are you?"

"Eighteen," the boy replied. "Are things at the Putilov Plant as bad as I've heard?"

"That's why I'm here."

"There he is—Father Gapon," said the boy, his gaze shifting to a tall, thin man with long, wavy hair and whiskers.

The man strode to the opposite side of the room and faced the crowd. He had an intensity in his demeanor, as if he were on guard. Conversations stopped and all eyes fell on the man who had organized the meeting.

"Welcome," Father Gapon began, folding his hands together in front of his chest. "It pleases me to see that word is spreading. This is double the number of men we had at our last meeting."

A few men raised their glasses and cheered.

Father Gapon waited patiently for the noise to cease before continuing in his smooth, tenor voice. He explained that the Assembly of Russian Workers had been started to defend workers' rights through peaceful methods. "At this moment in time, we have almost six thousand members and nine branches in Russia."

Glasses pounded on tables throughout the room and men roared their approval in unison.

"Enough talking," shouted someone from the middle of the room. "It's time to call a strike, to put words into action."

Murmurs of approval rippled through the room like water swelling around a stone thrown at just the right angle.

A thick-set man in front of Sergei raised his fist. "We need to show once and for all that we're not going to take this any longer."

Another man raised his fist. Then another, and another, until almost all the men at tables held their arms high, blocking Sergei's view of Father Gapon.

"Calm yourselves, men," called out Gapon, in a loud yet controlled voice. "All violence begets is violence."

Angry voices subsided as the men slowly lowered their arms.

"We will mobilize when the time is right. But we will never resort to violence," Gapon continued.

At the end of the meeting, Sergei elbowed his way through

the crowd of men to the door and went outside. He took a big gulp of air and leaned against the building until his heart slowed and his rapid breathing subsided. Then he headed back to the barracks and lay down. But every time he closed his eyes, he saw the madness of the Ekaterinoslav strike and remembered how he'd lost Lev during the commotion.

上海

"Another vodka," shouted Pavel, slurring his words. He held his glass up and grinned. His body swung precariously back and forth.

Sergei glanced around the noisy tavern, stuffed with Putilov workers commiserating the firing of four of their own, including Pavel. Sergei's vision blurred from the number of drinks he'd had, and he doubted his legs would even hold him up if he attempted to stand.

"They've got spies, I tell you," said Pavel. He tried to slam his hand down on the table but because of his intoxicated condition, his hand merely fell half-heartedly onto the wood surface. "They knew I attended Gapon's meetings. That's why they fired me."

"But I went, too," said Sergei. He leaned on the table to keep the room from spinning. "And I didn't get fired."

"Not yet." Pavel tilted his head back and poured vodka down his throat. He set his glass on the table. "Just you wait, your time will come."

"You're right." Sergei moved his empty glass in circles. In truth, he'd been surprised that he hadn't been fired. His fear was that he would be found out as a member of the Combat

Organization and sent to prison or to exile in Siberia. "I know that I'll be without a job soon."

"It's your face." Pavel leaned forward, so that his chin rested on the table, and squinted at Sergei. "You look too young to be dangerous." He paused. "Don't grow whiskers. They'll make you look old and mean."

Sergei ran his fingers across his stubbly chin. Though he'd shaved in the morning, facial hair had surfaced again.

"Promise me you won't grow whiskers," said Pavel urgently. "Because I feel responsible for you, like a big brother or uncle. And I don't want anything to happen to you." Pavel's words slurred together making them hard to understand.

"I promise I won't grow whiskers."

"And stay out of trouble. Forget Father Gapon. Forget striking."

Sergei shook his head which spun as it moved. "No, I can't do that. It's too important to give up."

"You must…" Pavel's voice faded. He rested his head sideways on the table.

Sergei reached across the table and shook Pavel's shoulders. "Wake up," he said groggily.

Pavel groaned but didn't move. Sergei searched for a familiar face to help him get Pavel back to the barracks. But the cloud of tobacco smoke and his blurred sight from too much alcohol, left him swaying back and forth, unable to recognize anyone. Sergei stood, but kept his hands on the edge of the table to keep himself steady.

Sergei stumbled over to Pavel and pulled his arm until Pavel lifted his head. Together Sergei and Pavel staggered through the over-crowded tavern, past other fired men drowning their sorrows in alcohol, past fellow workers drinking in support of their unlucky comrades.

The frigid fall air jolted Sergei from his stupor.

"What's going on?" said Pavel drowsily, his head hanging down.

"Just getting you to bed," answered Sergei. His warm breath made smoky wisps as he spoke.

"I'm not tired," said Pavel, his head swinging from side to side like a piece of rope dangling in the wind.

"That's what you think," said Sergei in a husky voice. He stopped for a second to catch his breath and resumed walking, his body hunched over under the weight of Pavel.

"Who do you have here?" asked the guard when they arrived at the barracks door.

"Pavel," said Sergei.

The guard checked something on the paper in his hand and frowned. "He was fired today, which means he can't stay here anymore."

"He just lost his job and has nowhere else to go," begged Sergei.

"That's the rules," said the guard. "I didn't make them. I just enforce them. Get him out of here."

"Where are we supposed to go?" asked Sergei. "It's the middle of the night. He can sleep in my cot and I'll sleep on the floor."

The guard shook his head fervently. "He's not allowed on the premises. Take him away or I'll be forced to report you."

Sergei looked helplessly at Pavel, whose bleary face showed no sign of comprehension. Sergei pivoted himself and Pavel around so that they faced the opposite direction.

"There's a bridge near here," said Sergei. "It's not perfect but it'll provide cover if it rains."

"You mean we're going to sleep under a bridge?"

"What other choice do we have?" Sergei trudged off, practically dragging Pavel toward the bridge, half a mile from the Putilov factory, on a secluded street.

His legs felt like jellied pork's feet when he finally reached the bridge. Sergei dropped Pavel on the downward sloping riverbank underneath.

He lay down on his back and listened to Pavel snore. The sound reminded him of his father who'd spent many days and nights on their sofa recovering from excessive drinking. *I'm becoming exactly like the person I detest more than anyone,* thought Sergei. *I swore I would never let drink get the better of me and now, here I am, spending the night under a bridge.*

He turned onto his side and eventually lapsed into a restless sleep, where he saw himself drawn as a caricature, passed out on the sofa in his Kishinev home. In his dream, his sister watched him with her round, sapphire eyes.

Part Five
Winter 1905

There is no good reason why we should fear the future,
but there is every reason why we should face it seriously,
neither hiding from ourselves the gravity of the problems
before us nor fearing to approach these problems with the
unbending, unflinching purpose to solve them right.

—Theodore Roosevelt, President of the United
States of America, *Inauguration Speech,*
March 4, 1905

27

January 1, 1905

Dear Sergei,

We just received our papers allowing us to travel to America, and are working extra hours to save money for a place to live when we arrive. We're booked on the SS Mongolia to San Francisco on January 6, which is hard to believe, after almost two years of dreaming about America. Can you believe I am sixteen years old and Menahem is now nine?

I'm nervous about traveling so far from Russia. Even after all we've lost, I still remember the good things like cherry blossoms in the spring, rooks cawing at daybreak, and the sound of my father's fiddle on cold winter nights. I also dread putting more distance between us.

The chance of you finding Menahem and me in such a big, unknown place as America seems as likely as finding lilacs in the snow.

Menahem is very worried about being so far from you. I'm afraid he will never be completely happy until he is with you again. We must keep writing, no matter what, for Menahem's sake.

I laughed when I received the caricature you sent with your last letter! The way you drew me and Menahem on a tiny boat bound for America is extraordinary. Are my eyes really that big? To be perfectly honest, I prefer this more informal style to the very straight and serious lines you drew before your accident. You should try and sell some of your sketches. They're as good as or better than the ones I see on advertisements and postcards.

I'll write with our address once we're settled. I hope you're well and that we may see each other soon.

Take care of yourself,
Love Rachel

"We're leaving soon, for America." Rachel spoke softly, as if unsure of her own words. She stood in front of Mr. Ezra's desk. The room hummed steadily with the sound of presses.

Mr. Ezra lifted his head and looked at her with unreadable eyes. He dropped his feather pen and folded his hands together. "Really?"

"Yes. It's taken longer for our papers to come, but they are now here."

"Good for you! Not so good for me."

"What do you mean?"

"You could be a good writer one day, one of my best."

Rachel blushed and twirled her braid. "I need more experience."

"You should go back to school to learn about history, science, and philosophy. You need to broaden your world so that you understand what's important, so that you see what others don't."

"I want to attend school more than anything," said Rachel. "I want to go to university. My father wanted that for me."

"You will, but promise me one thing," said Mr. Ezra.

Rachel nodded.

"When you arrive in America, ask advice from everyone, but follow your own mind."

"That sounds like something my father would say."

"He must have been a very wise man."

Rachel smiled.

"Keep a journal of your passage to America," said Mr. Ezra. "Send me a story. I can't promise I'll print it but..."

"I know."

Mr. Ezra rose and leaned forward, extending his hand to Rachel. She put her small hand in his and he squeezed so hard her fingers scrunched together.

"*Zay gezunt*," he said in Yiddish before letting go of her hand.

"Be well," she echoed, before turning and moving out the door of the *Israel's Messenger* for the last time.

上海

Baby Zelda clamped onto Shprintze's breast as naturally as if she'd been doing this for years, not months. She made little cooing sounds as she drank her mother's milk, her tiny fingers curled up against her mother's skin. Shprintze sat on her cot with Zelda and Rachel. Anna and Nucia sat in chairs facing them.

"I can't believe you're leaving so soon," said Shprintze. She pried Zelda from her breast, and lightly patted the baby's back. "I don't want to think about living here without you."

Tears pressed against the back of Rachel's eyelids. "I wish you could come with us."

"You know that's impossible now that we have Zelda. With me not working, we can't save any money for America."

Rachel nodded. "Any news from your husband, Anna?"

Anna's face darkened. "Only a short letter. He's exhausted after another ten-day battle." She sniffed and looked away. "Eleven thousand Russian men were killed this time."

"Thank goodness he's safe," said Rachel.

"For now." Anna paused and gazed at Zelda. "Every day I fear he'll be injured or worse. The thought of never seeing him again, of never having his children weighs me down inside. Sometimes, I can hardly get up in the morning."

"You can't give up hope," said Nucia. She reached over and gently stroked Zelda's head.

"I won't," said Anna.

"Zelda looks just like you," said Rachel to Shprintze.

"Do you think so?" Shprintze peered at her daughter's face. "I think she has Isaac's nose and mouth." She smiled at Zelda and put her finger on her tiny nose. "Would you like to hold her?"

Rachel nodded eagerly.

Shprintze leaned forward and placed Zelda in Rachel's arms. Rachel held her breath, afraid to move for fear of upsetting Zelda.

"She's so small," whispered Rachel, unable to pull her face from Zelda's, who looked up at her with a serious expression.

"You can move. She won't break," said Shprintze.

Rachel relaxed her shoulders. She touched Zelda's hand and Zelda immediately wrapped her fingers around Rachel's finger. "She's strong."

"I know, Isaac is so proud."

Zelda began making whimpering noises, and turned her head in Shprintze's direction. Rachel stood, and handed the baby back to her mother. Shprintze kissed Zelda's forehead and Zelda made cooing sounds again.

"It's amazing," said Rachel. "The bond between you and your baby, the love she has for you. It's wonderful."

"Someday you'll know what it's like, too."

"Maybe, or I might end up as an old writer with only my books to cherish."

"I doubt that," said Anna.

"I agree," said Shprintze. "You'll find a smart, handsome man in America."

"I might already have found someone," said Rachel, distracted by Zelda's cherubic face.

"What? Who?" asked Shprintze.

"Yes, tell us," urged Anna. She sat taller and turned slightly to look at Rachel.

"I can't tell you," said Rachel.

"Why not?" said Shprintze. She lifted her shirt and guided Zelda's lips to her breast.

"Because it's not proper, my friendship with him."

"What do you mean?" pressed Anna.

"You can't tease us with such a small morsel," added Shprintze.

"I wish I had better control of my mouth," grumbled Rachel.

"Well?" said Shprintze.

"He's not Jewish," Rachel blurted out.

Shprintze's jaw dropped open and Anna frowned.

"It's Sergei, isn't it?" asked Nucia.

"Yes, but I haven't seen him since I left Kishinev," Rachel continued. She tucked a piece of hair behind her ear. "I'll probably never see him again."

"I should hope not," said Shprintze. "Going to America will be the best thing for you. You must leave all thoughts of him behind."

Anna nodded her head in agreement.

"You should stop writing to Sergei," said Nucia. "How can you forget about him when you continue writing to each other?"

"I'm not ready to put Sergei out of my mind," replied Rachel curtly, putting an end to the conversation.

28

"Hire them back," Sergei chanted, raising his fist in the cold January air. He, along with thousands of other workers from all parts of Petersburg, had gathered at the Putilov factory demanding that the dismissed workers be rehired, and that the foreman who discharged them be fired.

"Give me back my job," shouted Pavel hoarsely. He stood beside Sergei waving a white banner with, "I want to work" written in red ink.

A light snow fell and dusted the men with flakes that melted soon after landing on their heads and coats. The workers stood in a cluster, converged in front of the factory gate. The doors had not opened once during the five hours they had been striking on behalf of their unemployed comrades. Even though the plant had stopped operating, with so many people refusing to work, management refused to respond to the crowd.

Fatigue weighed Sergei down. He dropped his arm and

glanced sideways at Pavel's face, carved with intensity and rage. Sergei resignedly lifted his arm again and resumed chanting until darkness fell at five o'clock. As he stood, numb with tiredness, Sergei felt as if he were being watched. He turned his head to the right. A swarthy man holding one end of a protest banner peered at him intently.

The man held a kerosene lantern beside his face, illuminating his prominent forehead. For a second, Sergei wondered why the man looked at him with such attentiveness. Then Sergei remembered. He'd seen this man the day von Plehve had been killed. This man must have recognized Sergei and knew he had been involved in the murder.

Sergei pushed forcefully through the crowd and bolted away from the factory. He peered over his shoulder and saw the swarthy man following him with a determined expression on his face. Not wanting the man to know where he slept, Sergei ran past the barracks and kept going, his head jerking from side to side as he looked for a place to hide.

The barren streets seemed forlorn and uninviting with many closed factories that sat unnaturally silent under the colorless sky. Sergei's right foot slipped on an icy section. He slid across the road, his feet spinning, out of control. He held both arms out to steady himself, regained his balance, and continued running. The sound of the man's footsteps behind Sergei grew louder. Sergei ran faster. He darted left when he came to a narrow, winding side street. Sergei glanced over his shoulder; the man had also turned onto this street.

"Dammit," said Sergei. His lungs were raw from running in the cold air, but Sergei pushed himself to go on. When the road forked in two directions, he went left and then took another left

turn so that he was actually running back to the factory. Sergei
wove his way through a maze of small streets until he heard
nothing behind him. He hid behind an abandoned warehouse
to make sure the man had gone. After waiting thirty minutes,
Sergei headed back to find Pavel, his heart pounding so hard
he feared it would burst.

"I don't want to strike anymore," Sergei announced to
Pavel when he found him at the tavern outside the Putilov factory. Pavel sat at a table with four other men from the factory.

"Then march with us and Father Gapon next Sunday," said
Pavel. "With him leading us peacefully to the Winter Palace,
change is bound to happen when the Tsar sees the crowd. I can
feel it in my bones."

"Let's drink to Father Gapon," said one of the other men.
He raised his glass of vodka and tapped it against Pavel's glass.

Sergei sat down, ordered a drink, and felt the tension
around his neck loosen as the alcohol circulated through his
body.

上海

It was Sunday morning, January 22, 1905. Snow blew fero-
ciously into Sergei's face as he marched with the orderly
procession along Dvortsovaya Street toward the Winter Palace.
Unlike the strikes in which only men took part, this peaceful
demonstration involved women, children, and even babies. An
icy wind from the Neva River whipped through Sergei's threadbare coat, chilling him right to his bones. Fifty feet ahead of
Sergei, Father Gapon led the way in a long black cloak, his tall
fur hat perched upright on his head. He carried a cross and a

petition signed by more than one hundred and fifty thousand people asking for a reduction in the work day to eight hours, increased wages, improved working conditions, and an end to the Russian-Japanese War.

Sergei moved alongside Pavel but, unlike the others surrounding him, he didn't carry an icon, a cross, a flag, or the Tsar Nicholas' portrait. He also refrained from singing religious hymns or the Imperial anthem, "God Save the Tsar." Instead, he moved grudgingly, his lips pressed together, casting his gaze throughout the throng of people.

"...protect the Tsar," sang Pavel, his voice slightly off-key. "Strong and majestic, Reign for glory. Forever our glory..."

"I can't believe you still think the Tsar deserves our support," muttered Sergei, once Pavel had finished singing the anthem.

"He doesn't know how bad things are," said Pavel. "When he sees us and listens to the words of Father Gapon, everything will change. The Tsar will take care of us."

"I think you're wrong."

"You shouldn't have come if you don't have faith in Father Gapon and Tsar Nicholas," said Pavel.

Sergei recalled a similar conversation he'd had with Lev on the way to strike at the Ekaterinoslav factory. A sense of doom unsettled Sergei's nerves. Though he worried about the outcome of this demonstration and continued to question whether the Tsar would ever be on the side of the workers, he had thrown in his lot with the marchers. As with the Combat Organization, there was no way out anymore. Sergei raised his fist and reluctantly joined in singing the Imperial anthem.

As they reached the Narva Gate leading into the Winter

Palace, Sergei glimpsed a solid barricade of Cossacks and *Hussars*, the cavalry with their tall, white plumes on their helmets, facing Father Gapon and his demonstrators. They had their rifles aimed directly at the crowd. Without provocation, without warning, the soldiers opened fire on the procession with bullets flying towards men, women, and children. Red stains appeared on the fresh snow before Sergei had time to think about what to do.

"Why are they shooting at us?" Pavel cried. He ducked and avoided a bullet that missed his head by an inch. "What the devil is going on? Where's the Tsar? Why is he allowing this?"

A bullet grazed past Sergei's ear. For a second, he couldn't move, couldn't speak, couldn't think. Another gunshot, followed by a man's jarring cry made Sergei jump. A soldier aimed at a nearby mother and child. Pavel leapt on top of them to shield them from a bullet. Instead it hit Pavel in the back.

"Are you all right?" shouted Sergei to Pavel. He raced over to his wounded friend and pulled him off the unharmed woman and girl.

"He saved our life," said the woman, pointing to Pavel and clutching the girl tightly.

"Get away, far away from here," Sergei yelled at the woman. "Go now."

The woman took one last look at Pavel, who groaned as Sergei held him under his arms and tried to pull him to safety.

"You're going to be all right," Sergei said to Pavel. He dragged Pavel past crumpled bodies and bloodstained snow. Blood gushed from the wound in Pavel's back and seeped onto Sergei's coat as they moved. Screams and cries tainted the air.

Bullets continued to fly past Sergei. He crouched low to

the ground and moved as fast has his legs could carry him, but it wasn't fast enough. A bullet hit him in the right arm. It felt as if his flesh was on fire. He dropped Pavel and fell to his knees, covering the hole where the bullet had entered his skin. Blood soaked through his coat, a crimson circle that grew until blood completely drenched his arm.

The screams of terror grew louder and bodies littered the ground like leaves falling from trees in October. Sergei peered at Pavel, whose face had turned ash-gray. He kneeled beside Pavel and listened for the sound of his friend's breathing. Nothing. Sergei looked at Pavel's chest to see it rise with life. It didn't move at all.

Slowly, Sergei got to his feet. "I wish you'd been right about the Tsar," he said with one last look at the dying Pavel, before shuffling through the Narva Gate, clutching his injured arm to his stomach.

29

Sergei sat on his cot in the barracks and struggled to get his sleeve over his bandaged arm. It had been two days since Gapon led them straight into the Tsar's bullets and more than a thousand people had been killed or wounded. Gapon had fled Petersburg and now the city had sunk into a decrepit chaos with looting, fighting, and destruction.

Sergei tried to figure out his next move. With his injured arm he couldn't work in the factory. He knew it was just a matter of time before he'd be thrown out of the barracks.

"Why didn't you tell me?" Sergei's foreman marched into the room, his face red and sweaty. He held a scrunched-up newspaper.

"Tell you what?" said Sergei. He stood and creased his brow.

"This, dammit, this!" The foreman slammed the newspaper down onto Sergei's cot and hit it twice with his hand.

Sergei scanned the headline. "Police Agent Nikolai Tatarov has betrayed members of the Combat Organization." Sergei grew faint as he continued to read. He saw his name listed in the paper along with the rest of the members of the Combat Organization. "This can't be," he whispered, reading further. Savinkov had denied any knowledge of the combatants or their activities.

"All this time while you've been working for me, you were involved with the Combat Organization," said the foreman, his voice rising to a shout. "They might think I'm a member. The police might come after me."

"No," said Sergei, filling his sack that held everything he owned—an extra shirt and pair of trousers, his sketchbook, and his letters from Rachel and his mother. "The organization knows nothing about my factory work. You're not in any danger."

"That's what you think. They have eyes and ears everywhere."

"I'm leaving now," said Sergei, tying his birch-bark pack shut and throwing it over his shoulder. "When they find I'm gone, they won't care about the factory or anyone I worked with."

"They'll question us, pressure us for information."

"I'm sorry."

"Just get out of here," said the foreman angrily, pointing to the door where men had gathered to listen.

Sergei brushed by the men and walked out of the barracks. Heads turned in his direction as he moved briskly through the grounds of the Putilov factory. He quickened his pace and kept his eyes straight ahead to avoid meeting curious stares. Seeing a trolley rolling slowly to a stop at the corner, Sergei broke into a run and jumped on. Just thirty minutes to reach the Vitebsk train station, he figured. Then, somehow, he'd have to travel across Russia without anybody discovering that he was, in fact, Sergei Khanzhenkov, member of the Combat Organization. A rebel and a fugitive.

I'll hide on a ship bound for America, he thought, scratching his head and tapping his feet. *Nobody can know my real name. I'll grow my whiskers and find a pair of spectacles to disguise my appearance.* Sergei recalled Pavel advising him never to grow whiskers and his lips curled up. *Even Pavel would approve of me with whiskers under these circumstances. It won't hurt for me to look a bit mean and old.*

Lost in thought, Sergei didn't notice a man get on the crowded trolley a few blocks before the train station.

"You," said the man triumphantly, halting in the narrow aisle and pointing at Sergei. "You were there the day von Plehve was killed."

All the color drained from Sergei's face when he recognized the swarthy man. He quickly pushed his way past the passengers and leapt from the rear door of the moving trolley, bruising his knee when he landed on the sidewalk. Looking up, he saw that the man had not been able to get off the trolley to chase him. Ignoring the throbbing pain, he limped along an alley behind a row of shops. A forest skirted the alley and the train tracks. Sergei moved into the stand of leafless birch and linden trees. Using the tree trunks to help support his weight. He hobbled to the Vitebsk train station, only to find it crawling with police and Cossacks armed with rifles.

They must be looking for members of the Combat Organization. I'm a fugitive now. From the forest, he watched the officers pacing in front of the station before turning his attention to the train bound for Vladivostok. Sergei sat on the cold, damp ground and examined his knee, which had swelled. He inspected the bandage on his arm and made sure it was secure. Then he waited.

After a very long hour, black steam poured from the train's engine, bells pealed, and the train rumbled forward. The reverberation grew closer and the ground started to shake as the train came nearer. Windows slithered past as train cars rushed by, gathering speed. Sergei, his teeth clenched as he put his full weight on his sore knee, ran as the train continued forward, until the last car drew beside him. He willed his legs to go faster and just before the car pulled ahead, Sergei jumped on the train. The force of the oncoming wind felt almost too much to overcome. Sergei struggled against the gale and wrapped his arms around the railing to secure his body. Immediately, he felt steadier and pulled his body against the train.

Looking back, he watched the station recede in the distance, the same impressive building he'd seen when he'd first arrived, so full of hope. Now, a wanted man, he was leaving in disgrace.

Cold and worn out, he began to doubt his chances of making it across the wide expanse of Russia this way. He thought about how he'd have to sneak aboard a ship, since he would never get identification papers now that he was a fugitive from the law. He thought about the determined faces of the police officers he'd seen at the train station and shuddered.

Sergei wrapped his fingers around the pouch on his waist, which bulged with the money he'd made drawing posters, and his eyebrows shot up with a plan. With the money in his pouch, he'd be able to bribe his way out of Russia. He would take a different route from Rachel and Menahem. Instead of heading east, he'd go south to Moscow. From Moscow he would head to Odessa, then across the Black Sea and into Turkey where he would no longer be in danger. Then, somehow he'd find a way to get to America.

Sergei tried to focus on the scenery rolling by, the outskirts of Petersburg fading into the countryside. But in his mind, Lev and Pavel's faces kept appearing through the birch trees. He kept thinking about how they had each risked and sacrificed their lives to make Russia a better place for its people. *Unlike them, I'm running away like a frightened sheep*, he thought. *I'm acting like a coward by running away, just like Papa said.*

He jiggled his money pouch. A hardened look settled in his face. Instead of leaving Russia right away, he could go to Moscow, where he was still unknown by the police. And there he would continue the fight for workers' rights—for the sake of Lev and Pavel.

Sergei's thoughts moved to Rachel and Menahem. They'd be on their way to America by now. He closed his eyes and imagined himself with them. He could see Rachel's face, radiant and pure, and Menahem's trusting, eager eyes. But Sergei could not see himself, only a murky shadow lagging behind Rachel and Menahem.

Sergei made his decision. It was not yet time for him to go to America. There was no place for cowards in America, the golden land of opportunity. But someday he'd get there, Sergei vowed to himself. As soon as his work in Russia was done, he'd be on his way.

30

Two men dressed in black, V-necked tunics with berets on their heads, stood on both sides of the doorway leading into the lowermost part of the huge ship, *S.S. Mongolia*. Four masts ascended the deck and a tall, black pipe was mounted in the middle of the ship.

This was the largest ship Rachel had ever seen and it made her feel very small. Holding Menahem's hand, she tried to be brave and looked straight ahead, following her sister and Jacob down a narrow, rickety staircase to the lower steerage area.

"Hold on tight, Menahem," she called out. "These steps are very steep."

In the gloomy interior, kerosene lamps, hanging from the sides of the boat, provided the only source of light. The air grew more stale with every step Rachel took. Perspiration, dampness, dirt, and dead fish filled Rachel's nose. She coughed and slowed down.

"Hurry up," came an angry male voice from above. "We haven't got all day for steerage passengers to board."

"Single men and women to the stern," said an authoritative voice from below. "Separate quarters for single men and women in the stern. Family quarters in the bow."

Rachel continued to descend the stairs until her feet reached a wooden floor. She stood in the bow of the ship, which spanned from one side to the other. Grimy portholes offered a hint of light. Narrow tables with benches attached to beams took a small portion of the bow; rows of bunks separated by thin iron rods consumed most of the space. A straw mattress, blanket, tin plate, cup, knife, fork, and spoon lay on each bunk.

Rachel watched people cram together onto the bunks. More than a thousand steerage passengers would fill the underbelly of the ship—too many people for not enough beds.

"How long will it take to get to America?" asked Menahem.

"Four weeks, maybe longer," said Rachel. "It depends on the weather."

"Maybe we should go back to Kishinev now," pleaded Menahem. "Maybe all the bad people are in jail and it will be safe, and we can find Sergei…"

"I wish we could go back to Kishinev, but we can't. Not now. Not ever." Rachel hugged him tightly.

A ship's attendant assigned them their bunks, located in the middle, between a Jewish woman and her three children, and a young couple with a baby. Rachel and Menahem took the top bunk and Nucia and Jacob lay down on the one beneath. Though she felt exhausted, Rachel could not sleep in such close quarters. The woman beside her smelled of sour milk, and Rachel couldn't stop thinking about how sick she had been on the much shorter passage from Vladivostok to Shanghai.

Before the ship left the harbor, Menahem drifted into a fitful sleep, and Nucia and Jacob spoke softly to one another. Rachel climbed down from her bunk and made her way carefully up the steps to the deck of the ship where she breathed fishy sea air. Only a tiny square of deck space had been reserved for steerage travellers, roped off to separate them from higher-class passenger areas. Ironic because there were three times more steerage passengers than first- and second-class combined.

Huddled between other steerage passengers, Rachel gazed at the shore where people had gathered to watch the ship depart. A tall man waved exuberantly, two women wept, and a family peered anxiously at Rachel, as if searching for someone. Rachel remembered the day they had arrived in Shanghai for the first time—the day they had been forever separated from their mother.

Living in Shanghai has been bittersweet for me, thought Rachel. *Losing Mother yet gaining a brother in Jacob. Working in that horrid laundry yet gaining valuable writing experience with Mr. Ezra. Becoming as close to Shprintze as if we were sisters, yet having to say goodbye. I will never forget my time here, but I'm anxious to leave.*

A warning bell rang out and a moment later the ship began to slither away from the dock. Rachel kept her eyes on land as the vessel picked up speed and glided through the water. A heavy woman stood nearby with five little children begging to be picked up. A young couple held hands, their faces pale and taut. A dozen or so passengers lay closely together, babies cried, children whimpered, and others called out for people who did not answer.

The people on shore grew smaller and smaller until they became specs in the distance. Shanghai's large and colorful vista disappeared over the horizon. Rachel, standing tall in spite of the severe wind which chapped her skin and numbed her cheeks and lips, remained on the deck until her toes became so cold she couldn't feel them.

The steerage deck swarmed with people. Some, like Rachel, sat lethargically after violent bouts of seasickness. Others played cards, and a few sat and listened to a spry old man play his violin. The warm, soothing sun lulled Rachel into a light sleep. She dreamt she was back in Kishinev, sitting in front of the stove while her father played his violin. She smelled her mother's black bread, saw her father's beguiling smile, felt comfortable and safe.

Only when the weather suddenly changed, when the sea began to swell, tossing the ship to and fro, did she wake and realize her dream was not real. She descended the stairs to get away from the stranger's violin that had carried her back to a time that no longer existed.

上海

The midday bell sounded and the steward beckoned the passengers for dinner. Rachel hadn't eaten in two days, but her empty stomach had grown more resilient now, more adjusted to the sudden pitches of the ship. She left her bunk and joined Menahem, Jacob, and her sister at the crowded table.

"Are you sure you should eat, Rachel?" asked Nucia, who had taken to life at sea surprisingly well.

"I'll have a little food and see how it settles." Rachel caressed her raw, sore stomach.

A thin soup was ladled out of a filthy bucket. Rachel dragged her spoon through her bowl and found small pieces of potato and carrots and something lumpy she couldn't define. The lukewarm broth reminded Rachel of the meager, tasteless soup she'd eaten every day after the Kishinev riots. She emptied her bowl and sat back to wait and see if it would stay in her stomach.

Fragments of conversations speckled the air—a mother, speaking in Yiddish, admonishing a child to eat, a husband and wife speaking in hushed tones about money problems. Three men arguing about the time it would take to get to California. Privacy did not exist. Every word, every breath echoed throughout the bow.

Remembering Mr. Ezra's words that she should write about her experience, Rachel brought out her journal. On the deck, she began to write.

There are so many people like us on this ship. I cannot help but wonder where they're all from, what they've been through, how they came to be here, and who they've left behind. Though I am glad to be on the way to America, my bones ache for my friends who could not come with us. I wake up every day worried that they have been hurt, or worse.

The days in steerage are intolerably long. Today I stayed in my bunk, except for meals, and escaped the dreariness and bad smells by sleeping. This is what most of us do in steerage. There is very little room for anything else, not even garbage, which covers the floor along with vomit that has not been cleaned. I wonder how the other passengers in first and second class, above us, spend their time. In the evening, I hear music and thumping from them. Perhaps they are dancing?

The babies are crying now. I can hear them all the way here on the deck. Once one starts, the rest join in, like a symphony of sobs that does not end for hours. I miss the quiet in our little house, the privacy I used to have to read and write. On this ship I feel like a caged animal.

Rachel's stomach growled with hunger as bread and butter arrived at their table. It had been two weeks since they'd left Shanghai and her body had finally adjusted to the violent waves that tossed her insides like fall leaves in a windstorm. She reached for a piece of the bread but not quickly enough. Greedy, soiled hands appeared from nowhere, grabbed viciously for the bread like wild animals, as if they had not seen food in months. Men's hairy, ropy fingers, women's bony, ashen hands, even children's stubby knuckles joined the battle for food.

In the end, Rachel managed to get two small pieces of bread, slightly torn at the corners, for herself and Menahem.

"I'm not very hungry," said Nucia, who had not managed to get any bread. She stared at Rachel's piece and licked her lips.

"We'll get extra next time," said Jacob, eyeing Rachel's bread.

"I can break my piece into three," offered Rachel. She tore it into thirds and handed a piece to Jacob and another to Nucia who devoured the bread in one gulp. Rachel threw angry looks at the people who had taken two pieces each.

The next morning, her stomach hollow and growling, Rachel joined the fray, pushing and grabbing until she had four large pieces of the bread. She handed bread to Menahem, Nucia, and Jacob without a word.

上海

Rachel turned on one side and then the other, but could not get comfortable. She sat up.

"Is it morning, Rachel?" mumbled Menahem.

"No, I just can't sleep."

"Me neither."

Rachel surveyed the almost silent area. Whispering, she told Menahem to follow her. Carefully, she got off her bunk and crept toward the stairs with Menahem close behind. As she ascended the staircase, the cool air cleansed her face.

On the steerage deck, a few men lay snoring. Rachel put her finger over her mouth and silently led Menahem toward the ladder past the roped-off steerage deck. They started climbing until they were on the upper deck.

"Where are we?" asked Menahem.

"Sh. We're on another part of the ship, where the rich people stay, but we have to be quiet."

He nodded, the whites of his eyes gleaming in the moonlight.

Rachel took his hand and strolled along the deck, doing her best imitation of the confident, well-to-do women she'd seen in Kishinev. The broad, white deck had rows of comfortable steamer-chairs set against the upper-class cabins. Light streamed from brass-rimmed ports and a woman's soprano voice resonated through the air. The singing ended and loud clapping ensued.

They walked farther along the deck, past a smoking room, where the smell of tobacco poured through the crack under the closed door.

Rachel stopped outside a lit port, knelt down beside Menahem, and peered through the clear, round window. A handsome, well-lit room appeared, with the widest bed Rachel had ever seen. A floral-patterned cover embellished the bed, and a desk, chair, and a long velvet sofa had been placed neatly on the opposite side of the room.

"Who sleeps here?" asked Menahem.

"I don't know…"

"Hey, what are you doing?"

Rachel bolted up and found herself face to face with an astounded watchman. He held up his kerosene lantern, almost blinding Rachel with its bright light. She grabbed Menahem's hand, told him to run, and took off back the way she'd come, dragging Menahem behind her like the tail of a kite. The watchman followed them all the way to the ladder that led to the steerage, huffing loudly. Rachel shoved Menahem down and scrambled after him, her heart racing. They stooped under the rope dividing the steerage from the rest of the ship and hurried down the stairs to their bunks.

"Pretend to be asleep," she told Menahem, when they jumped into their bunk.

Five minutes later, the watchman came down the stairs and shone his lantern around the bow. Apart from a few women nursing their babies, the area seemed quiet. The watchman grunted and went back up the stairs, muttering about obnoxious steerage passengers.

Rachel smiled, turned on her side and fell asleep, dreaming about flowers and big beds, and warm, comforting light.

31

February 20, 1905

As I near American soil, I am proud to be amongst so many brave and loyal Jews. I have seen how their stead-fast faith has led them here to a new and safer world. I have seen them hold onto their faith in the darkest of times, clinging to it without question, with absolute trust. Yet, I now see that it was not our faith that put us in such danger in Russia, but our differences, our refusal to become Russian in culture and language, our refusal to conform to other expectations.

Though I want to keep my faith, I'm torn by my need for acceptance. I want a fresh start in this new world, to be seen as Rachel, an ordinary person, not as Rachel, a Jew. I want to be able to be Jewish without being defined as a Jew. I want to be an American.

—from Rachel's Journal

Rachel's heart skipped a beat when she heard the ship's horn announcing their arrival in San Francisco Bay, California. It had been six weeks since they'd boarded, and she feared she'd never feel land under her feet again. A sudden, powerful jolt almost knocked her journal out of her hands. She picked it up and followed Nucia and Jacob to the stairs leading up to the deck. Rachel tightened her grip on Menahem's hand and grabbed the stair railing to regain her balance.

"We made it, Nucia," said Rachel. "We're in America!" Nucia gave Rachel a big hug.

Rachel took a deep breath. Anticipation, excitement, and terror rose from her toes to the top of her head. Rachel almost felt as if she could fly, as if anything were possible now, because she'd come so far.

"Steerage will be the last to get off," announced the steward from the top of the stairs. "Could be hours."

A groan erupted from the passengers. Nucia and Jacob turned and waited for Rachel and Menahem to descend into steerage again.

Rachel's elation plummeted. She shrugged at Menahem. "I hate traveling in steerage," she said, walking down the stairs and climbing back onto their cot.

"When I'm big and go on a ship, I'm going to stay up there." Menahem sat beside her and pointed upwards.

"Where will you go?" she asked.

He scrunched his mouth and thought about this for a moment. "To Petersburg, to find Sergei."

上海

Almost three hours after the ship had docked, steerage passengers were allowed to go up to the deck. A fog enveloped Rachel as she stepped outside. She squinted through the haze. Wide lumps rose from the bluish-green water. *Small islands?* She could just make out the skyline, something like Vladivostok's hilly, rugged landscape. Tall buildings dominated the view, with the occasional steeple jutting high into the sky. Further inland, hills transpired above the buildings, looming in the background like shadows.

"You're on board until you've passed a medical check," the steward called out, cupping his mouth with both hands.

"You can't be serious," said a father of six little children, all in various stages of distress. He held a small boy and girl in each of his arms.

"San Francisco has had a deadly epidemic of bubonic plague," the steward replied. "Carried here by ship. These people aren't taking any more chances."

Rachel's legs grew weak as she listened to this conversation. They'd come so far, all the way across the Pacific Ocean, only to be met with apprehension and fear that they were carrying a disease.

Rachel glanced over her shoulder at the deep, greenish-blue water that had carried her to America and vowed she'd never go back. She sat on the deck with Menahem, Nucia, and Jacob and settled in to wait for the medical exam. Rachel gazed at San Francisco, rising above them like tall birch trees over her home in Kishinev. She knew in her heart that she had finally realized her dream. Had they been alive, her parents would be relieved to know she had made it to America where Jews weren't hunted down like foxes or deer.

"You have kept your promise," Nucia said softly to Rachel. "You brought Menahem to America."

Rachel shrugged. "With Jacob's help."

"We're all family now," said Jacob. "We help each other."

"Our father would have liked you," Rachel said to Jacob.

"I wish I could've known him," said Jacob with a sincerity that moved Rachel.

"In a way, you do," Nucia said. "Rachel is very much like our father, strong-minded, curious, and smart." She turned, facing Rachel. "We wouldn't be here without you."

"That's not true." Rachel shook her head. "We need each other, just like Jacob said. I don't know where I'd be without your patience."

Nucia smiled and rested her head against Jacob's shoulder. This subtle warmth reminded Rachel of Sergei. Would he ever make it to America? Would he even be able to find them? Or would he eventually forget about her and Menahem?

"You're thinking about him, aren't you?" asked Nucia, interrupting Rachel's thoughts.

Rachel lifted her eyes to meet Nucia's. "How did you know?"

"You get a faraway look in your eyes when you do. It scares me."

"What are you scared of?" Menahem asked Nucia. "San Francisco?"

Nucia opened her palms and looked to Rachel for the answer.

"No, San Francisco doesn't frighten Nucia," said Rachel slowly. "She's just nervous about our future."

"Do you think something bad will happen to us in San Francisco?" asked Menahem.

She peered at the unfamiliar city, and was filled with optimism and trepidation. "I don't think it will ever get as bad for us here as it did in Kishinev."

"It will be hard at first," added Jacob. "Learning a new language, finding jobs, and a place to live…"

"But once we're settled," said Rachel, cutting in excitedly, "we will build new lives for ourselves in San Francisco."

"We can't forget who we are and where we've come from," said Nucia looking solemnly at Rachel. "We must live in a way that honors our parents and our faith."

"I think they'd understand if we change our customs a little to fit into America," said Rachel.

"We didn't come all this way to give up our identities."

"No, but I don't expect to live exactly as we did in Russia, thousands of miles away," argued Rachel. "I want to learn English, to go to school, to become a writer. I want to do things I couldn't do in Russia because I am a Jewish girl."

"Traditions are all we have to keep our memories alive, to keep from losing our way in this new world."

Rachel got to her feet, undid her braid, and ran her fingers through her long, wavy hair. "There are many things I want to forget. The things I want to remember are inside me forever." She fixed her gaze on San Francisco. "I don't need to act a certain way to remember who I am or where I've come from. When I step off this ship, I intend to look forward, not back. I will become an American."

Historical Note

Rachel's Promise is set against the backdrop of actual historic events: the historic movement of Russian Jewish refugees to Shanghai at the beginning of the twentieth century, the Russo-Japanese War from February 8, 1904 to September 5, 1905, the assassination of Interior Minister of Police Viacheslav von Plehve by the Social Revolutionary Party's Combat Organization on July 15, 1904, and the massacre of "Bloody Sunday" in Saint Petersburg on January 22, 1905.

While wealthy Sephardic Jews first arrived in Shanghai in the late 1800s, the Russian pogroms created a second wave in the early 1900s. Shanghai allowed all people to live there without identification papers, and though the Chinese essentially kept to themselves and there was a language barrier, Jews were treated well. A Yiddish newspaper called *Israel's Messenger* was published monthly by Edward Ezra, and the Shanghai Jewish School was built in 1900 by D.E.J. Abraham. The Sassoons and the Hardouns, successful Jewish families, built grand hotels and mansions in Shanghai, and offered charity services to Jewish refugees escaping from Europe and Russia. Still, it was difficult for many Jews, such as Rachel and her family, to earn a decent living in Shanghai. This was the main reason why many refugees left Shanghai for the United States and Canada, where there was more space for living, there were more opportunities for work and education, and burgeoning Jewish communities of immigrants from Eastern Europe flourished.

Most of the events within this novel are true and many of the characters in *Rachel's Promise* actually existed: Interior Minister Viacheslav von Plehve, Father Georgiy Gapon, Boris Savinkov, Edward Ezra, Yosef Trumpeldor, and Dora Brilliant.

Thousands of Jews fought in the Russo-Japanese War and were injured, killed, or missing in action. The Social Revolutionary Party organized strikes for better working conditions and pay, including a massive strike at the Putilov factory that paralyzed Saint Petersburg for days. The Combat Organization, an offshoot of the Social Revolutionary Party, set factories on fire and plotted assassinations of government officials. It was responsible for the killing of Interior Minister von Plehve.

Father Gapon, a Russian priest, was an enigma to all, with his refusal to be paid for his work, and his disdain for traditional Russian Orthodox views. Ironically, Gapon was enlisted by the government to organize workers' associations throughout the country. He held meetings throughout Saint Petersburg with police pretending to endorse these events; behind his back, the police were arresting people who attended these meetings.

In an attempt to gain the Tsar Nicholas II's support for

workers, Gapon led thousands to the Winter Palace, January 22, 1905, where they were attacked by the Tsar's army. This was called "Bloody Sunday," a brutal massacre, which killed or wounded over one thousand people. It was a turning point in Russian history since it proved to ordinary Russian citizens that the Tsar had no concern for them. This eventually led to the Russian Revolution of 1917, the downfall of Nicholas II, and the end of the Russian Empire.

Please note that some place and road names have changed since 1903, the time of this story. I have endeavored to use the historical names of the time. Also, the use of Saint Petersburg and Petersburg is interchangeable, Petersburg being used more commonly in speech.

Rachel's Promise was inspired by my grandmother, Rachel Talan Geary, who fled to Shanghai after escaping a massacre in Russia with her family. She attended school in Shanghai and took English classes after finishing high school. In 1927, she boarded a ship for California alone, worked as a nanny in Oakland, and attended the University of California, Berkeley. She graduated in 1930 with a degree in science.

Glossary

Blini: Small, light pancakes served with melted butter, sour cream and other garnishes.

Boker tov: Hebrew for good morning

Challah: A Jewish braided bread eaten on the Sabbath.

Chupah: A canopy under which a bride and groom stand during a traditional Jewish wedding ceremony.

Cossacks: Russian soldiers belonging to a certain ethnic group; in the late nineteenth and early twentieth centuries, the Tsarist regime employed Cossacks to provide police services such as preventing pogroms and suppressing the revolutionary movement.

Cracknels: Hard, crisp biscuits.

Fen: A Chinese coin worth one-hundredth of a *yuan* or one-tenth of a *jiao.*

Gan-eyden: Literally translated as the Garden of Eden, a paradise some Jews believed in for the afterlife, not necessarily Adam and Eve's Garden of Eden.

Hussars: Horsemen, much like cavalry, with colorful dress uniforms. Most Russian hussars wore red breeches.

Jiao: A Chinese coin equal to one-tenth of a *yuan* or hundred *fen.*

Kaddish: A prayer recited by mourners for the dead.

Kiddish: A blessing to sanctify Shabbat.

Kopeck: A Russian coin. In 1704, Russia was the first country in the world to introduce a decimal system, where 1 *kopeck* is worth one-hundredth of a *ruble.*

Kuetya: A sweet grain pudding; often the first dish in the traditional Russian Christmas Eve supper, made of wheat berries, poppy seeds, honey, nuts, and raisins.

Kugel: A baked Jewish pudding made from egg noodles or potatoes, often served as a side dish on the Sabbath.

Kvass: A non-alcoholic, fermented drink in Russia made of black or rye bread.

Mikveh: A bath used for ritual immersion in Judaism, to regain purity.

Pastils: A sweet medicinal pill that dissolves in the mouth.

Pirozhki: Baked or fried ravioli-like buns stuffed with fruit, vegetables, or meat.

Pogrom: A Russian word for persecution or massacre.

Provodnitze: Train conductor.

Ruble: A Russian coin or note worth one hundred *kopeck*.

Sampans: A long, flat-bottomed boat with ends that curve up and often some kind of roof for shelter.

Shabes: Yiddish word for the Jewish Sabbath, the most important day of the week (Friday) for Jews. It begins eighteen minutes before sunset and ends on Saturday night about forty-five minutes after sunset. For observant Jews, no work or active pursuits, such as writing or tearing paper, are allowed.

Shtetl: A Yiddish word for a small town with a significant Jewish population.

Shul: Another name for synagogue, where Jews worship and study.

Smetana: heavy dairy product like sour cream.

Sochevnik: Christmas Eve holy supper.

Socialist: One who advocates public ownership of industries, resources and transport.

Versta: Obsolete Russian unit of length defined as 500 *sazhen* (3,500 feet; 1.0668 kilometers)

Yuan: A Chinese coin that equals ten *jiao* or hundred *fen*. One *yuan* is worth five rubles.

Zay gezunt: Yiddish for "be well."

Acknowledgments

Rachel's Promise and my first novel, *Rachel's Secret*, are inspired by the lives of my maternal grandmother, Rachel Talan Geary, and her sister, Anna "Nucia" Rodkin. Though my grandmother died when I was twelve, her spirit and resilience fill the pages of this book. Nucia, who lived to see my first child, spent hours one hot afternoon in Montreal telling me about her family's life in Russia and Shanghai. I told her I wanted to write a book one day, so that my children would understand the sacrifices their ancestors made in order to survive. I wish she and my grandmother were here today to see my words in print.

To my mother, Ann Geary Sanders, for her infinite support and for the memories of her mother she shared with me. To my father, Richard Sanders, for spreading the word about my books at every book store he enters, and for his daily phone calls which remind me to take a moment and breathe. To Gayle Geary, for her steadfast encouragement and for giving me my grandmother's 1930 class ring from the University of California, Berkeley. To Sharon Rodkin, for the gift of Nucia's trunk which she brought from Shanghai in 1947, carved with images of the old city walls.

Much appreciation to author Ibi Kraslik and the University of Toronto's Creative Writing Program, which helped me make the leap from cautious journalist to inventive author.

I am grateful to Margie Wolfe and Second Story Press for believing in me and *Rachel's Promise*, and for providing me with such a wonderful editor, Sarah Swartz. Sarah's attention to detail and her extraordinary organizational skills not only improved the book, they showed me how to be a better writer. A big thanks, also, to the Ontario Arts Council for the generous Writers' Works in Progress Grant.

About the Author

SHELLY SANDERS was born in Toronto, Ontario, moved to Illinois when she was eight, and back to Canada for high school. She graduated from the University of Waterloo with an Honors degree in English, Ryerson University with a graduate degree in Journalism, and has just completed the University of Toronto Creative Writing Certificate program. Before turning to fiction, Shelly worked as a journalist for 20 years, with articles in many of Canada's major publications including *Maclean's*, *Reader's Digest*, *Canadian Living*, the *Toronto Star*, *National Post* and *Today's Parent*.

Shelly's first book—*Rachel's Secret*—was inspired by her grandmother's escape from Russia. *Rachel's Promise* continues to follow her grandmother's path as she fled to Shanghai where people of all races and faiths were accepted without papers in the 1900s. Shelly has received a substantial grant from the

Canada Council for the Arts to write the third book in The Rachel Trilogy, which will be published soon.

Shelly lives in Toronto with her very patient husband, three amazing children, two dogs, and two lizards. Visit Shelly online at www.shellysanders.com.